# THE CROWN OF CONSEQUENCE

# THE CROWN OF CONSEQUENCE

## KAITLYN MUELLER

Kaitlyn Mueller

Dedicated to my husband who has been the best support system anyone could ever hope for.

THE KINGDOM of MELTED COR
SELINDA'S HOUSE
THE MARKET
COR PALACE
JERICHO

# THE CROWN OF CONSEQUENCE

The Sequel to The Crown of Misfortune

The day was dreary. The waves didn't stop rocking the boat. I thought I had hated sailing before, but this, this was unmanageable.

"Are we almost there?" I shouted through the howling of the wind. The rain had picked up again, drenching us from all sides.

"Almost!" shouted Helena.

We had been on the boat for six days now; I wanted to jump off. I sat with my back against the side of the boat as I dropped my head onto my knees and cried. The weight of it all was coming down on me. I'd lost Dova, my tea shop, my life, and now we had to find some sort of miracle in order to somehow beat the king. I felt defeated. Dealing with anxiety my whole life meant constantly overthinking about little things, but this was actual danger.

"Ever, it's ok. I can see the shore from here."

Mikka's calm voice steadied me. It was just six days ago that he had kissed me. He had kissed me every day since. I felt grounded when he was there. I looked up, nodded, and since I had nothing left right now to say, I just smiled. I felt like I would puke if I even tried to open my mouth again. The rocking was relentless. Gregorio and Bondi directed the sails, trying to bring us closer to the coast.

"Jericho!" Helena shouted.

I had never seen Jericho before. After all, it was in a different kingdom. A kingdom feared by most.

The Kingdom of Melted Cor.

A queen had ruled their kingdom ever since its king had tragically died, although most people say she actually killed him. I had heard that she was unforgiving and literally melted the people that defied her (and the people that she just didn't like). We didn't have time for new enemies now, so we were just looking to go in, find the answers we needed and head straight back to stop King Jett.

I didn't even bother wiping the tears off my face, and it was raining too hard for it to matter anyway. I started to stand up to see what Mikka was referring to, but the rocking of the boat almost knocked me off of my feet. Mikka held on to me tightly. Fern came up to us from behind and grabbed my hand too. She was so little but so brave, and I was glad to have her here.

I looked to the shoreline: it was rocky, with tons of boulders protruding from the ocean. The waves crashed down onto them as if trying to push them back under the sea, and I wondered how we were planning on getting to shore in this storm.

But I'd have to worry about that in a bit. Bondi and Gregorio were trying to keep the boat steady, doing their best to steer us toward the shore, and my stomach turned again. I leaned off the side of the boat to puke. If only Gregorio wasn't exhausted and could use his gift to push the wind. The storm continued to rage, as if it were trying to punish us, and the thunder roared as lightning surrounded us. A huge bolt of lightning flashed, and suddenly the mast broke in two.

"Everyone hold on!" Gregorio shouted as he tried to channel the last bit of energy he had to redirect the boat with his gift.

The waves pushed us towards the shore, and it took only a few seconds for the boat to smash against a rock, cracking the hull. I tried to hold on, we all did, and I screamed for the rest of them to come together. The boat was going to sink, and I didn't know how to swim.

"Helena, Bondi, Gregorio, here!"

We knew it was over. We all held hands as the waves continued to smash us into the rocks, until the side of the boat gave way and we all plunged into the icy water. The current pulled me under immediately, but I would not let go of Mikka and Fern's hands. I could feel everyone trying so hard to hold on to one another, and caught a glimpse of Helena as she got up from under the wave. She managed to get in a gasp of air, and she let go of everyone and started swimming as hard as she could to shore. I kept swallowing gulps of the sea water, causing me to choke.

I could feel the panic attack starting to rear its ugly head. My heart was pounding, my chest was heavy. I felt myself slip out of everyone's hands. I couldn't swim. This was it. I tried so hard to move my arms, but I kept going further underwater. Down, down, down. The water started to fill my lungs. I couldn't breathe.

The current slammed my body into the large rocks, knocking the wind out of me. I kept reaching out, trying to grab for someone, anyone – but there was nothing to grab. The darkness started to creep in, and I could feel that I was losing consciousness. I didn't want to give in to it, I kept trying to flail my arms through the water, to try and swim, but the current was too strong. The water slammed my body back into the rock again, and I started to see little stars surround what was in my view. The darkness enveloped me, and everything went black.

I awoke on the shore of what must have been the coast of Jericho. I had to assume it was that, because I didn't think there was any other land out here. The water was still, so the storm must have just ended. The sun's rays shone on my skin, warming my freezing body from being in the water so long. I had no memory of what had happened, but I was sure I was lucky to be alive.

I tried to sit up as my surroundings came into focus. I looked around and didn't see any of my friends. I was completely alone. Being alone never usually bothered me, but this felt different. I had people depending on me, and I had started to depend on them. I felt the panic coming in and tried to push it away, like the waves push the sand away as they roll onshore.

I realized that my axe was gone, and so was the boat. There were small wooden planks lapping up against the shore around me, and I was sure that those were part of what used to be our boat. I pushed myself to my feet, trying to wipe the sand and dirt off of my face and out of my hair. I noticed that my hands were covered in blood now – my head must be bleeding from being slammed against the rocks. I wiped the blood off onto my wet clothes and moved closer to the water. I needed to get the dirt, blood and sand off of my hands, so I could properly wet my hair and clean my wounds. I tried to get as much water on my head as possible to wipe off all of the grime. It stung, but it would have to do for now, until I could find a place to get properly clean and wrap the wound. It wasn't a big cut, but big enough that it was going to keep bleeding if I didn't clean it out and bandage it.

I began to look around. The ocean stretched as far as the eye could see, not a ship in sight, nor could I see the land of the kingdom we'd come from. Behind me stretched a long plain, leading to mountains in the distance. I knew the stories: inside the valley between the mountains was the Kingdom of Melted Cor. I also knew to avoid going there at all costs. Even in our kingdom, their queen was feared. Our king was scary but not unpredictable, while their queen was completely unhinged. Just thinking about her sent a shiver down my spine.

I started to walk across the beach toward the plain, hopeful that I would see my friends in the clearing. Helena had told us we were going to the coastal town that she grew up in, but I didn't know this area so I wasn't entirely sure which direction to go in. I felt like I needed to lay down––the pain was unreal, my whole body aching––but I wanted to find my friends first. So I walked onward, looking everywhere. Still, not one of them in sight, and what was even weirder was that there wasn't anyone in sight at all.

The sand made it hard to walk fast. My shoes were wet and the sand sticking to them made them feel heavy. But I was afraid that if I took them off right now and then needed to run later, I would be much slower than usual. So I continued forward, to where the edge of the sand stretched into a grassy plain.

I couldn't see the town that Helena had talked about. It was nothing but empty land. I started to think about what this place looked like on a map and remembered that there was quite a distance between the towns on the outskirts of the kingdom. But I didn't know if I was north or south of Jericho. I wanted to continue to avoid the mountains, so I decided it might be best to walk the coast, to see if I could find any sign of anyone. My stomach growled, and I wondered how long it had been since we crashed. I wondered how far I had ended up from all of my friends.

My mind suddenly went to Mikka. I felt panic: what if something had happened to him, or Fern, or any of them? I quickened my pace, starting to run along the coast despite the thick sand. I ran for what felt like miles but it all still stretched to nothing. I slowed my pace down to a walk.

"MIKKA," I shouted into the empty nothingness.

No answer, no noise. I needed to eat something and find a water source that wasn't saltwater. The sun was so hot I felt delirious. I was exhausted. I decided to walk inland a bit to see if I could find any food or water. Straying from the coast wasn't ideal, but I didn't think that there was another option. I knew if I drank the saltwater I would get even more dehydrated, so I needed to find another water source and quickly.

I could see a tree line up ahead, just past the grassy plain toward the foot of the mountains. The forest had always brought me comfort, and it would be a good place to set up for the night if I couldn't find Mikka or any of the others before sunset. Setting up to sleep on the shore would provide me with no shelter and no coverage anyway, so this was a better option.

I headed through the plain toward the trees. It was a long walk, but one I needed to do. It had been hours since I awoke on the shore, and the heat and hunger had started to make me feel weak. But I had to keep moving if I was going to find food. I also wanted to make a healing tea, but without my supplies that wasn't happening. So I pushed myself to move faster, to get to the tree line quickly. I felt exposed in the open field, and while I knew it was a great way for my friends to find me, I also knew it was a great way for people I didn't want to find me too.

The tree line was finally within reach. I looked up at the massive trunks and took a big, deep breath. I liked the comfort of being surrounded by the forest. The large trees would provide shelter and a way to hide from anyone that I might not want to come across just yet. If I wasn't completely lost and separated from my friends, this would have been a beautiful place to set up a new life. It reminded me of home.

*Home. Kinver.* A place I realized I might never see again.

I let out a sigh and headed into the coverage and (hopefully) safety of the woods. It was a dense forest, but didn't look much different than the forests outside of Kinver. Similar landscape and foliage. The storm had left the greenery quite dewy, which meant I would be likely to find a water source from the rain.

One thing that really stood out from what I was used to was the leaves. They were massive, larger than cooking pots, whereas back home they were much smaller and duller in color. These leaves were such a bright green that they almost looked a bit fake.

One of the trees shortly ahead had these massive, bowl-like leaves stretching all the way down it, even onto the trunk. I reached out to grab one and a ton of water poured out of it onto the forest floor. Jackpot. I reached over toward the next leaf and carefully put my lips up to the edge, so that I could slowly pour some of the freshly caught rainwater into my mouth. I drank as much as I could – the heat had really dehydrated me.

Next, I started to search the forest floor for anything that could be eaten. Mushrooms, bugs, moss, anything that could provide me with just a little fuel and nutrition for the time being. There were lots of mossy areas where mushrooms had sprouted through the earth, as well as small shrubs with berries that I had never seen before. I gathered some of each and sat with my back against a large tree trunk so that I could look more closely at them before deciding what to eat. The land was different here, and just because something wasn't poisonous at home didn't mean it wasn't in Jericho.

I pulled apart the mushroom. It looked so much like the edible ones in the forests back home, and I knew that without food I'd starve, so I decided to eat them later. I wanted to heat them first though, just in case. The berries, however, were green on the outside and bright purple on the inside, making me think I didn't know enough about them. My hunger was pushing me to eat them, because of how good they looked, but I would be no good to my friends if I died from eating poisonous berries. I couldn't take the risk, so they would stay behind. I just had to shake temptation a little longer.

I finally felt hydrated and had enough energy to start gathering logs for a shelter. There were two big trees nearby, so close to one another that the gap between them would make a good spot for a little fort. I wanted the protection since I was alone, so I started stacking logs on top of one another, propping a few more up at an angle to build my little structure.

"C'mon, just a few more," I said out loud to myself, for encouragement. I wanted to get the fort set up while it was still light out.

After the logs had been properly set up to give me a little coverage, I grabbed some moss and filled in the cracks, in case it got colder during the night. Once the cracks in the wood were taken care of, I took a step back to look at the whole thing. It was very minimal, and honestly wasn't my best work, but I was hoping that it would only be for one night anyway.

I gathered some small logs to get a fire started, since the sun was starting to set and I needed to eat something. I grabbed two pieces of wood and tried to will a fire, but I was weak so I ended up having to try and start my fire the human way. I rubbed two sticks together for a while, trying to get a spark, and was finally blessed with a flame. I was able to use the fire to get warm and dry off my cold, wet shoes and clothes.

I pushed my mushrooms onto the end of a stick and roasted them over the fire. The slightly burnt texture tasted weird, but it was better than nothing. As the darkness set in around me, the fire became my only source of light, and I put some protective wards around my makeshift home. Adding some more wood to the fire, I got into my tiny fort. It was damp, but I was tired, so after a few restless moves, I finally fell asleep.

**3**

The howls in the distance woke me.

I slowly opened my eyes and saw a canopy of stars shining through the trees. It was still nighttime but at least I'd been able to get a little sleep. I didn't mind being alone in the woods at night, most of the time it was actually comforting. This time, though, I was in totally new territory, with no idea what had happened to my friends, and it all felt a little frightening. I could tell that the sun would be up soon so I decided I'd get my fire going once more to keep my mind busy until then.

I grabbed a few logs and twigs that I had gathered last night and tried to get a spark going. After a few sad, unsuccessful attempts, I finally got a flame. The warmth of the fire woke me up a bit, and I was able to take in my surroundings with the light that the fire provided. I grabbed some more of the mushrooms that I had found last night and roasted them to make a quick breakfast.

I wouldn't be able to stay here long – I was in uncharted territory in a kingdom I knew nothing about, and I'd need to hurry to find my friends so we could get home. King Jett would use the Book of

Viemprosoon enough and we would be in a world of problems if we didn't get ahead of him. He might have even used the book by now, in which case we were all doomed already.

The sun started to rise above the tree line. The warmth of the fire and the food in my belly made me feel like I was ready to start moving back to the shoreline. I grabbed some more water out of the large, bowl-like leaves to drink, and used some extra to douse my campfire's flames. The last thing I needed was to accidentally start a massive wildfire which would not only destroy the forest, but also give away my location.

Grabbing a rock with sharp edges, I decided that I would mark trees every few feet, so that I could find my way back here safely if I couldn't find any of my friends. That way, I wouldn't have to start over completely if I needed another day to look for them. With my plan decided, I headed away from the safety and density of the trees as the sun rose and walked back towards the ocean. I took in my surroundings as I carefully and quietly made my way down to the shore. It was really beautiful here. The beaches were so much nicer than the ones back home, with a lot finer sand and fewer little rocks.

I knew that I had plenty of time to get farther along the coast today, which would hopefully give me more opportunities to run into Mikka and everyone else. I wanted to make the most of the daylight, which was why I was out so early, hoping that I would see a sign, any sign, of the others being alive. I was also on the look-out for anyone else that might be looking for me, whether that was King Jett, the people of this kingdom, a random stranger, it didn't matter. Anyone could be a threat at this point, and I would treat everyone that way just in case.

It felt lonely, walking through the plain uncovered and unprotected by my surroundings. But I still couldn't see anyone around for miles, which was both a good sign and a bad one. I was aching to see another person, especially if it was one of my friends, but I also had a looming feeling within that if I came across a stranger, they were going to try and hurt me. It made me nervous. But, as far as I could see, there was nothing, literally nothing, for miles.

I decided to head left along the coast. It was a different direction than I had come from, so I hoped to see a town or a shack or anything that would give me a clue as to where my friends might have gone. I took my shoes off to walk along the beach, the sand soothing on my feet, like a little massage with each step. After a rough few days, the walk in the sand was needed, even with the worry and doubt still crowding the back of my mind.

The sound of the waves crashing on the shoreline before settling back into the ocean was enough to drown out my thoughts and allow me to focus on each step, constantly looking around in case there was danger. It also allowed me to be extremely quiet as the sound of the waves drowned out the tiny sound my footsteps were making on the sand.

As I continued looking as far ahead as I could see, I kept thinking how weird it was that there wasn't a small town or anything like Helena had described. I couldn't have washed ashore that far from where we were trying to land. I felt like maybe our coordinates had been wrong all along, and maybe this wasn't the side of the island we needed to be on. As I looked closely at the horizon ahead of me, the thought that maybe I alone had washed up on this shore, and that the others were on the other side of the island, crept into my mind. I pushed it aside though, because now wasn't the time for fear to overtake my thoughts.

I kept walking. Onward.

I must have been walking for hours. The sun had changed positions from low in the sky to straight overhead, signaling to me that it was around noon. In the distance, I could see something small that was getting larger with each step toward it.

"Finally," I whispered out loud.

It was a small house, built at the edge of a marsh. I decided to get close enough to take a look at who lived there, instead of just walking up to knock on the door. Luckily, there were large boulders protruding from the sand where the marsh met the beach, so I walked up to one and hid behind it. Trying to see what was going on from this far away was difficult, and I wished I had my binoculars with me. But I had to try anyway; I couldn't just hope someone would have good intentions, especially in a kingdom I didn't know anything about.

Up close, the small house looked well lived-in. There was a little garden right outside which looked like it was regularly tended to, surprising considering this was literally the only home I could see in the area. The house was just far enough away from the ocean that it wouldn't get swept into the sea, but close enough that the view must have been important to whoever lived there. Or maybe they just wanted to be as far as possible from anyone else? It didn't seem like there was a town within eyesight, so the person might simply like to be alone. I could relate to that.

I wasn't sure if any of this information could help me decide whether the person who owned this house was inherently good. After all, they might be out here because they had been exiled. Either way, my guess was that they wouldn't have a way of reporting me immediately to anyone, and they were so far out that it would at least give me time to run.

I was honestly out of options. It was either check the house or go back to the forest and try again tomorrow. I'd have to come back here eventually.

I decided to ask for directions, or at least find out where the nearest town was so I could scope it out. I wanted to find my friends, get a boat and get the heck out of here before the king found us. I approached slowly, with caution, constantly keeping my head on a swivel to watch my six. The house was surrounded by a small wooden fence with tons of panels missing – it looked like the fence hadn't been looked after in the same way as the little garden had. I pushed the small door of the fence open and approached the hut. Walking up the two steps to the front door, I took a deep breath in.

"Here goes nothing," I whispered to myself. I slowly put my fist up to the door and knocked twice. "Hello? Is anyone home?" I said softly.

I heard the creak of floorboards from inside the house, giving away that someone was definitely home. My heart started pounding out of my chest, the steps sounding closer with each passing moment. The doorknob slowly turned and the door swung inwards.

"Hello," a soft voice said from inside.

An old hand reached out to grab mine and swiftly pulled me in.

My heart was racing in my chest. The wrinkled hand that had pulled me in belonged to a very old woman. She closed the door quickly behind us and hurried herself into the kitchen. She moved so quickly that I didn't even have time to get a good look at her. But I was certain she'd be back.

I was standing in the stranger's living room. The inside of the house was old, but very well cared for. There was no dust or sand anywhere; it looked like the old lady had taken a lot of pride in keeping her home clean. I looked around, alert, trying to see if there was anyone else here but it seemed to just be her, judging by the lack of sound.

The only thing I could tell just from her hands alone was that she had to be at least eighty. The shelves on the walls had small picture frames that contained pictures of her and another woman about her age, except she was much younger in those photos. In fact, all of the pictures were of her and that woman, and I wondered where the other woman was.

"Girl, you must have a death wish if you're out on these shores alone. Someone could have seen you," she said from the other room.

"I'm not alone," I said sternly back at her, trying to believe my own lie. I figured it was better to lie right now than to get caught up in her thinking that I didn't have anyone looking for me. I walked closer cautiously, trying to see if I could get a better look at her and the inside of the house.

"Well, whether you're alone or not, you're alone right now. And wandering these parts alone, even if only for a little bit, can get you killed. Or worse."

The tea kettle on the stove whistled, interrupting the woman's next words as they were drowned out by the loud sound. I peeked my head into the room, but there was nothing noticeably alarming or that made me think I was in immediate danger. I felt like I could breathe out.

The woman poured hot water into two cups, adding lemon, honey and a few other spices. *Tea.* I missed tea. It had been weeks since I'd had some, and warm tea would feel so great right now.

As she walked over to bring me the tea, I got a better look at her: she was tiny, had short gray hair, and her face was covered in wrinkles that showed her age. Her green eyes looked sad, like they had seen things that couldn't even be described. She was wearing tan pants and a light-colored knitted sweater that was slightly frayed, but not enough that she couldn't still wear it.

The woman gestured over to a small high-top table with two chairs. It looked like that was the only seating she had, so I guessed she didn't get company very often. She put the cups down on the table and sat down in one of the chairs, so I followed and sat in the other. I was still frantically looking around to study the rest of her home – although I felt safe, you could never be too cautious.

"Relax. I'm not going to hurt you," she said as she sipped her tea.

I looked down at my own mug, at the steam rising from within.

I put my hands around it to feel the heat, and my whole body felt instantly warmer. I lifted the cup to take a sip, and as I put it back down, I found myself looking at her home's decorations. Everything was very old, nothing new at all, including those pictures of her and the other woman. The wallpaper was peeling off of the walls slightly in some spots.

"Now dear, tell me about yourself," the woman said as she continued to sip her tea. "Why are you alone?"

I looked at her. "Like I said, I'm not alone. I just lost track of my friends and came down to the shore to see if I could find them. My name is Evana." I let my voice trail off to hide my lie and took another sip my tea. I didn't know if I could trust her just yet, so I wanted to keep my identity hidden.

"Evana, is it?" she said. "I am Selinda. Welcome to my home. You're more than welcome to stay here while you wait for your friends. It isn't safe out there for you to be wandering about on your own." She looked down at her cup and then back up at me with those sad green eyes. Her kindness was comforting, but I was sure it came with a cost. Everything comes with a cost, especially safety.

"Selinda, thank you for that kind offer," I said, "but I have to continue onward. I actually don't know where my friends are or even if they'll be passing through here, so I really can't wait." I had decided to share a little bit of truth, in the hope that she would tell me if she had seen anything. "Did you happen to see anyone pass through here? There would have been five of them. Two girls, one very little, and three men." I took another sip of tea, watching her facial expressions to see if she would reveal anything to me.

She only looked up at me with a desperation in her eyes. "No, can't say I have seen them, but you cannot continue venturing on your own. It's not safe here." She looked out of the window.

I didn't like the way she'd said that. I wasn't sure if it was the fact that her voice trailed off, or the way she looked away, but something about it sent a chill down my spine.

"What do you mean it's not safe here?" I asked, eager to know more.

Instead of answering right away, she slowly got up out of her chair and walked over to the window. She closed the curtains before walking back to her seat, shaking her head. "You must not be from here," she said. "The queen is dangerous. She doesn't take prisoners, she just kills people when it best fits her agenda. This kingdom is plentiful: lots of varieties of crops, plenty of food, clean water. But she claims it all belongs to her. You have to send in a list of all the food and water you have, anything you bought, and if she thinks it's too much, she kills you or someone in your family as punishment." Her voice was getting quieter and quieter. "If you're here without permission, you'll get a one-way ticket to the castle, and 'one-way' is the key word there. You won't return. She'll simply decide if you're worthy enough to work for her or if she wants you dead." She sipped her tea, her tone totally matter-of-fact. Like it was the only way they had ever been living here.

My heart was pounding. What if my friends had been sent to the castle? We had to stop King Jett before he figured out how to manipulate the dead. We had to find a way off this island kingdom to get back to our own. But I couldn't stop thinking about my friends being in trouble. My breath started to shorten, my panic attack creeping back into existence. The pressure on my chest felt enormous.

Selinda could tell something was wrong. She got up and put a hand on my back as I struggled through my panic attack.

I tried to take deeper breaths, to ground myself into this space. I wanted Mikka. Now more than ever, to comfort me. But the thought of him made things worse. The room was spinning and I felt like I couldn't quite catch my breath. So I sat and focused on my inhale, trying to get it deeper. I counted to five, and then counted to five on my exhale. I worked to slow my breathing, to focus on my current space.

After a few minutes, the world started coming back into normal view. The pressure released from my chest and it felt like I could breathe normally again.

"It's ok, it will be ok," Selinda said.

Her voice was comforting. She reminded me a bit of Dova, which made me feel horribly sad but also at peace at the same time. We sat in silence for the next few moments. I finished up my tea and placed the cup back down on the small table. I felt quite embarrassed. I mean, I didn't even know this person and yet here I was, sitting in her kitchen having a full-blown panic attack. I had to get over my-self. After all, there were way worse things than Selinda thinking I was weird for having an anxiety attack in her house.

"Thank you. For understanding," I said, and she nodded. I wanted to change the subject. "Tell me more about yourself Selinda," I said to her. "Who's the other girl in the photos?" I wanted to know more about the person that had taken me in for the day, this stranger who lived so far away from the castle and any civilization.

Selinda looked down at her mug. There was a small look of happiness on her face, coupled with discomfort. She took a deep breath before she spoke.

"That was Elavane. She was my partner. My wife. We used to live in the marketplace, above one of the shops just outside of the castle. We had a small farm stand. It was years ago, but it feels like a lifetime. The queen herself would come into the market, collecting money, lists of what was bought, sold, eaten. She... " Selinda paused. Tears started to fill her eyes, and she took another deep breath. "Elavane, well, she was stubborn. She didn't want to pay the queen half of what we made, she said it didn't make sense to her. I tried to stop her from arguing, but she refused to give the queen her money.

And the queen, she's a Potens. She has the ability to heat things... until they melt... " She stopped.

"You don't have to continue if you don't want to," I said, seeing how much pain she was in from sharing her story. I could fill in the blanks from here, and my eyes filled up with tears, knowing what would come next.

"No," she said. "I must share it, because if I stop speaking of her, eventually people will forget my love for her. The queen melted Elavane in front of me. Right after it happened, I moved out here, away from all the madness. I couldn't stand it any longer. That had to be fifty years ago." She walked over to a picture of her and her wife. "You see, if you move out of the city, and out of the kingdom's reach, you don't have to pay half of what you make. But you're also not allowed to get anything from anyone still living there. I've been doing just fine on my own, with a view of the ocean that I know Elevane would have loved."

Something about her story was really bothering me, and although I wanted to comfort her, I had to get answers. "Wait," I said, confused. "Fifty years ago? So wouldn't the queen be old now too?" I hadn't heard anything about the kingdom choosing a new ruler.

Selinda looked back at me. "One would think. But, somehow, the queen still looks just like she did then, young and ruthless." She put the frame down, lost in remembering a life she had once lived.

But how could the queen not have aged? Everyone aged. Everyone had to, even Potens. Sure, there were some that aged slightly slower, but I'd never heard of someone not aging at all. Fern was the only thing close to something like that, and that honestly still worried me. Confusion filled my head, but I needed to make sure Selinda was alright after sharing that story.

"I am so sorry for what happened to your wife," I said. "I too know what it's like to lose your family to people in power. I come from the Kingdom of Aureum Ignis. My friends and I are here to get something that can stop our king,"

I was nervous to share this with her, but I had decided that she could be trusted. So I continued to tell her our story, the trials we had faced to get here, our long journey. I told her of Jett and the book he possessed. I told her everything except our real names, or what we were capable of. Especially Fern. She drank tea silently while she listened.

"We could take you with us when we go back," I said to her.

She shook her head. "No. I cannot leave the land where my love was laid to rest. But I am happy to help get you out of here if you find your friends."

"Thank you," I said as I walked over to the window, to look around the closed curtains. "You've been so kind to me. But I must keep going. I must find them first, before someone else does."

"If you want to go out and look for them, at least wait until nightfall," Selinda said to me. "Creatures don't lurk this far from the forests or the mountains, and you won't be as likely to be seen. You do not want to be seen." I nodded.

She walked me over to her couch to rest while the sun was still up. We agreed that I would leave at nightfall and get a little sleep before heading out. She kindly laid out a pillow and a blanket for me on the couch, which was a huge step up from my small fort the night before. The comfort and warmth of her home felt so much better than the forest floor.

I could sleep for a little while here. I felt in my gut that I could trust her.

"Thank you," I said as I tucked myself into the blanket. "I'll have to find a way to pay back your kindness."

She nodded and walked away, back into the kitchen. I drifted off to sleep.

S elinda was standing over me when I startled awake.

"Get up girl, they are coming," she said.

I sat right up, alarmed, my heart racing out of my chest. "Who's coming?" I asked. Selinda was quickly gathering my things for me, while I was still trying to process what was going on.

She said nothing, just grabbed my arm and pulled me toward the back door. As we hurried through the house, a loud knocking started at the front door. The sound of knocking alone made my anxiety go through the roof, but there would be no time for that right now, we just had to keep moving. My heart started racing faster.

"Who is that?" I whispered to Selinda as she handed me a glass bottle of water and a small bag filled with food.

"You don't need to find out, you just need to go," she said. "Head back down through that field out there. Stay close to the road, but not too close. I think if your friends are here, they will have headed into town to find you. Go now, and good luck." She pushed me out of the house.

I didn't even get a chance to thank her before the door quietly shut behind me. I hurried into the field, wanting to create as much space between me and her house as I could. The grassy plain didn't offer much coverage but it was still dark, so I hoped that if I hurried I wouldn't be seen. I tried to stay low, to avoid being seen by the people gathered at the front door.

I could see a few carriages parked at the front and side of the house, but I couldn't really make out what they looked like. I didn't have any clue why people would be here this late, so I just hoped that Selinda would be alright. The idea of her being alone with them made me nervous, but I didn't even have anything I could use to help defend her. And if I got caught, well, who knew what could happen then.

The moon illuminated the area around me enough that I was at least able to see where I was going. Selinda had said to stay close to the road, so that was what I aimed to do. I could see it in the distance but kept looking back at the house, trying to listen for any strange noises. But there was nothing. I feared what was ahead, but I was certain it was better than whoever had turned up at Selinda's house in the middle of the night.

As I ran as fast as I could toward the road, I felt guilty again for leaving her there alone. I kept thinking about whether I should go back, but I knew that if I got caught and the king used the book of Viempro, we would have a lot more to worry about than some strangers in the night.

I continued to run into the darkness as the trees in the distance started to get closer and bigger. I could hear the carriages that had been at Selinda's house heading this way, so I quickened my pace. I didn't know whether they were coming for me or if they were just headed in this direction, but I didn't want to take any chances and find out.

Maybe Selinda had told them about me. It made me feel sick to think it, because if she had, then I'd told her too much.

I darted into some thick shrubbery, into a place where I would be hidden. The anxiety was creeping back in – I didn't know what lurked in these parts and I was far, probably hours away, from my make-shift shelter. This was a new part of the forest. I found a few large bushes to hide behind, so that I could see the road but was far enough away that anyone passing wouldn't see me.

The carriages were getting closer and closer. I waited. And waited. My heart was pounding out of my chest, and I was scared the sound of my heartbeat was so loud that they might be able to hear it from the carriages. But they passed without stopping at all. It seemed they were headed toward the town. I didn't even peek out to see what the carriages looked like or how many people were in them, I just stayed hidden.

My heartbeat steadied as I heard the carriages getting farther away, and I started to take in my surroundings. The density of the forest, combined with the moonlight shining through the small openings in the canopy above, made it all look quite peaceful. I knew it still had to be early in the night because I hadn't slept for that long at Selinda's. I sat against a tree for a moment to look at the bag Selinda had given me. In it were a few pieces of assorted dried fruit, a handful of mixed nuts and some small bags of tea. I felt grateful. This would hold me over until I found my friends. I hoped.

Based on what Selinda had said, I decided to keep moving while it was dark. I just hoped she was all right – I'd have to find a way to pay her back for her kindness if she was ok. I tightened the bag, took a sip of water and headed out into the depths of the forest. I ran quietly into the darkness, thinking of Mikka as the familiar feeling of anxiety swelled in my chest. What scared me most was what my fate would be if I were to get caught, but I also knew that I had no choice but to deal with my fear. I had to push aside the nervousness and allow myself to just focus on the task at hand. I would have all the time in the world to worry later. But for now, I had to keep going. There was no other choice.

I was truly alone.

The woods swallowed me up as I moved further into the depths of the forest for cover. I could still see the moon peeking through the small gaps in the trees above, giving me enough light so that I was not completely without sight as I moved forward. The sounds around me intensified as I focused my attention on where I was going: I could hear the shifting of the forest floor as wildlife scurried about; I could hear the animals of the night, calling out to one another; I could hear the crunch of the ground under my feet as I moved swiftly forward.

I stayed in the densest part of the forest as I followed the path heading into town, hopeful to find some sign of my friends. I continued like this for what felt like hours, walking swiftly but steadily enough to not tire me out. I knew the journey would be a long one, but after having eaten and slept for a bit, I felt so much more alert.

Eventually, the darkness started to fade and the sun rose to take its place. As my surroundings came to light, I could see that the forest of the night wasn't so different from any other forest. Forests had always felt like home to me, and while I didn't love spending my nights alone in a completely new place, I felt as if I knew this area in the daytime, even if it was still unfamiliar. I felt alive when I was alone in the woods, and I felt the pressure rise off my chest, as if I could breathe a little deeper.

The thick foliage brushed against me as I moved through the forest. I felt small twigs leaving little scrapes on my arms, but there was no time to be cautious of what I was hitting – I had to keep moving through the brush. We were running out of time in this kingdom. We needed to get back to stop King Jett before he destroyed all that we knew and loved. And he would be coming for Fern.

*Fern.*

She was in danger. I had to move faster, I had to find my friends before anyone else did. I couldn't possibly stop the king on my own.

I quickened my pace.

I could finally see buildings in the distance. On the outskirts was a marketplace, filled with small tents and tables and all sorts of little local booths with different types of food, clothing, things to trade. There were a ton of people walking through it, making their purchases of the different products.

Even from back here in the tree line, I could see the walls of the Kingdom of Melted Cor. They looked like they were made of steel or something, and there was a massive metal archway that shone brightly in the sun; It became almost blinding if the sun hit it in just the right way. It was quite futuristic, almost as though it didn't seem real, but what surprised me most was that it didn't look to be guarded, which was very strange. But the marketplace was filled with people, so surely I'd blend in and could look around. It wasn't like anyone would be looking for me except my friends (I hoped).

I pulled the small bag around me and headed out from the trees into the marketplace. It was noisy. The sounds of people shouting "Fresh fruit, get your fresh fruit here!" and "Only ten balos, that's all!" and more echoed as I walked through. Ten balos was expensive for fruit. Fires crackled where small business owners were cooking meat to sell; the air smelled like cinnamon and bacon, vibrant. I felt my stomach grumble.

But I was able to blend in, so it didn't seem like anyone was actually looking for me here. I wandered each row, hoping to see a sign of my friends somewhere, but there was nothing. Only the growling of my stomach getting louder and louder until I couldn't take it anymore. I opened my small bag to grab some of the dried fruit – I didn't have anything I could trade for better food, so this would have to do for now. But having used all that energy to run through the forest, I was so hungry still.

As I walked past the endless rows of little tents, something bright almost blinded me. I blinked my eyes and looked around to see what it was.

*My axe.*

"What the…" I said out loud. That got the shopkeeper's attention.

"Do you need something?"

I looked up to see a tall man in purple and gold robes. The fabric that lined the robes looked to have actual gold twine woven into it, so it was clear he was wealthy based on his clothes alone.

"I was just wondering where you got that beautiful axe?" I said, trying to play it cool and not give away that it was mine.

"What's it matter to you?" the man replied.

"Well, I had a friend a while back that had one like that," I said, "and he said they were hard to find. So I was just wondering how I could get one." I took a small step back, making a little more space in case I needed to run.

The man looked me up and down and nodded. "Well, the funny thing about this axe is that I found it washed up on the shore, along with the parts of a broken ship. And the thing about broken ships is…" The man's voice trailed off as he took a step closer. He looked over my shoulder and nodded. "Broken ships are usually the ones that contain spies from the Kingdom of Aureum Ignis."

My heart dropped into my stomach. I tried to turn around, but two guards suddenly grabbed my arms and forced me to my knees on the ground.

"Makes me wonder what someone like you is doing, worried about an item like that?" the shopkeeper said as I tried to wrestle myself free.

"I just was curious, that's all!"

He lifted his chin and laughed. "Well, we'll see what the queen has to say about that."

The guards tied my hands behind my back. I tried to refuse to walk, tried to pull away from the guards, but they just dragged me by my arms without a care in the world. I wasn't embarrassed at being pulled along through the marketplace, but I was frightened that they had the axe and that I still hadn't found my friends. They couldn't prove that I'd done anything wrong though, since all I did was ask about the axe, and I didn't have to admit to anything.

The guards dragged me through the silver archway that separated the marketplace from the city, not giving me the chance to really look at it. Being pulled by my limbs wasn't really the way I wanted to explore this city, and I wished I could have studied the archway for a bit longer. The city was actually incredible this close up. The buildings were huge, stretching all the way to the sky, and it hurt my neck to try and look all the way to the top from way down here, especially as we were moving fairly quickly. The architecture was so different from back home, so much more industrial. The glossiness of it all was what really took my breath away, it was like seeing something from the future come to life. I had heard stories of this place, but none of them had described anything like this, and I was honestly blown away by the vastness of it all. I wanted to look around at the city, get a better view of the architecture.

I also wanted to plan an escape.

"Can you... stop for one moment, please?" I said. I tried to stand still, but the guards were moving so fast that I couldn't catch my footing. One of the guards looked to the other and nodded. They stopped moving so quickly that it threw me off balance.

"Thank you," I said as I struggled to my feet. I wiped away the dust and dirt that had accumulated on my pants from being dragged. The guards went to grab my arms again, but I pulled abruptly away from them. "You don't need to hold me, I'll walk with you," I said, taking a step back. "After all, I don't think I'm going to be getting away from you anytime soon."

I wasn't going to tell them that the first chance I had to run, I would take it. They could find that out the hard way.

But the reality was, I was outnumbered, in a city I didn't know at all, without any Potens help whatsoever. The thought of that worried me, but I couldn't let it stop me. The guard nodded but said nothing. One of them stepped behind me, the other stepped in front, and we continued onward through the city.

I quickly looked at my surroundings, both trying to take it all in and find any way to escape. The buildings that towered over us were bigger than any I had ever seen, and their shiny silver exteriors meant that they all reflected one another, causing a blurring effect and making it difficult to see clearly. As we walked, I kept watching both of the guards too, peeking over my shoulder to see the one behind me, so that I could see what they were looking at – people don't realize how obvious they are sometimes when looking at things, so I figured there might be a possibility that one of the guards would look at something that could help me escape.

The further into the city we walked, the more the fear swelled in my chest, making me feel like a panic attack was coming on. I had heard many stories of this kingdom's queen, and although our king was scary, she had always sounded way worse. I struggled to push those thoughts down so I could think of an escape plan, when all I wanted was to sit down and regroup. I needed time and space to figure out what was really going on here and how I could get away, but the guards wouldn't let me stop. Any time that I slowed my pace, they pushed me on through streets, making people stare. I tried to hear what people were saying, any hints of where I was going to be brought, but my thoughts were drowned in whispers of nervousness.

I couldn't help thinking about what Selinda had said, that seeing the queen was a one-way ticket, that there was no escape. I realized that even though I hadn't done anything wrong, it was very possible that the queen would decide to punish me anyway. After all, I was trespassing in her kingdom.

The two guards kept pushing me forward. The further we got from the market, the wealthier the people around me started to look. Ragged robes changed to silks and leather-bound shoes the deeper inside the city walls we went. Even the cobblestone road looked a little unreal and ethereal, paved with the same silver rock-like material that the arch seemed to be made of. I kept looking around, still trying to find a way out of here. There *had* to be something, because I knew that the closer we got to the queen, the more difficult it would be to escape.

The road finally stopped winding and led us down a straight path to a very large building. It reflected everything around it, just like the other buildings in the city, and this one shot so far up into the sky that it merged with the clouds and made it hard to see the top. The road got smaller and smaller as the building got closer and closer, becoming the only thing in my view. Massive front doors stretched twenty people high, plain in detail but incredibly shiny.

There were the biggest doors I had ever seen. I could also now see that the metal-like walls were embellished with intricate details, patterns that had been carved in to interrupt the smoothness of the outside. I would have loved to know what the patterns meant or why they were there, but I doubted anyone would give me historical information at a time like this.

Plus, I really should have been less worried about the design of the building and more focused on where we were headed, because I realized now that this sky-reaching structure was at the heart of the city.

The guards moved closer to me, tightening my surroundings until it felt like I couldn't breathe. One of them grabbed hold of my arm.

"Not so tight," I said. The guard grunted and held tighter.

There would be no time to escape. Everything was too close – I was drowning on land. As my anxiety surfaced and all of the feelings of panic caved in on me, the doors opened. They opened without a touch, showcasing a cathedral-like room that didn't match the exterior of the building at all. It looked like an old castle that had just been redone on the outside, to hide what it actually was: the queen's castle, the Cor Palace.

Dread filled me, worse than before, that tightness overwhelming me instantly. I felt like I was going to be sick. Not now. The anxiety made me stumble. But I couldn't show what I was feeling, I had to appear strong. I did not have time to panic right now.

The guard grabbed my arm to stop me from falling over. "No need to faint so soon, we're not even there yet," he said with a smile as he pulled me up.

We continued to walk down a large hallway and I took a deep breath in, trying to move past my panic attack. Part way down the hall, the guard touched the wall in a specific spot and a dark, dreary staircase appeared in the brick as the wall shifted into itself. The passage had a weird smell to it, almost moldy. The guard in front led the way and the one behind me nudged me forward, forcing me to head down the staircase.

I was sure that this was leading me to my death, but still I kept looking around to see if there was any way of escaping. I knew that when the time came, I would need to run as fast as possible and it would be difficult to retrace my steps to get out of the building. But with each step down the staircase my heart sank lower and lower, as I began to completely lose hope that I would be able to escape whatever fate this was leading me to.

I just hoped my friends weren't also in the castle. If we were all caught, then King Jett would take over and the world would be doomed. At least if they were safe and something happened to me, they could continue on with the plan. Even though I knew that meant they wouldn't be able to come and save me. But that didn't matter: I wasn't important, and my friends couldn't risk putting the fate of the entire world on the line just to save me.

I looked around one more time to see if there was any sign of an exit or another passage. But there was nothing. It looked like I would have to continue toward whatever end was waiting for me.

At the bottom of the staircase, the passage opened into what looked like a dungeon. There were small water moats between the cells and the main platform, filled with snapping animals that I had never seen before. They had incredibly large teeth and long, almost snake-like bodies that had gills on the sides. They were quick-moving, slithering like snakes but even more graceful. If I hadn't been absolutely terrified by them, I would have liked to examine them (from a distance!)

I looked around at the other prisoners, which took no time at all – although there were a huge number of cells, there were only two other prisoners. I wasn't sure if that was a good thing or a bad thing. Was the queen as terrifying as people made her seem, or was it all just stories made up to make people fear her? I couldn't be sure, not now at least.

The door opened in the farthest cell from where we were standing. No one had touched it, so it must have been someone's gift. I looked around, not entirely sure what to do, and the guard looked at me, nodded and pointed to the open cell. The moat between the cell and the platform we were standing on was wide, creating a pretty big gap with no walkway.

"How am I supposed to cross the water?" I said in confusion. If I jumped, the creatures beneath might get me. And while I wanted to look at them, because I'd never seen anything like them, I didn't want to be close enough for them to eat me.

"Not my problem. Get in," the guard said firmly, letting out a small chuckle. He pointed at the cell again, making sure I knew I didn't have a choice in the matter. I would have to jump. He pushed me forward, trying to get me to hurry up.

I watched as the creatures swam beneath, snapping at me out of the water. Up close, their teeth were way bigger than I'd thought. I didn't have the power to do anything with my gifts in a short amount of time, like freeze them. If I had a moment to brew some tea, I could have put the creatures to sleep so I could cross into the cell, but I didn't think the guards would be kind enough to get me what I needed and wait while the tea brewed.

I watched and watched as they swam, waiting for the perfect time to jump. They didn't have a particular pattern though, which made timing it incredibly difficult. Finally, I just started to count-down in my head. One, two, THREE. I jumped. One of the creatures leaped out of the water and snapped down hard, missing my foot by less than an inch. I landed hard on the cold, rock-like floor of the cell. My heart was racing, but I'd made it.

The door to the cell shut behind me, locking me in. Even though

I was relieved that I'd made it into the cell alright, I was still unsure of what would come next now that I was here. The cell was damp and I knew I would be uncomfortable, but I also didn't want to have to jump back over the moat.

"How long until I see the queen?" I shouted at the guards as they started to walk away. They said nothing, just continued to walk, leaving me and the two prisoners in our individual cells. My panic attack finally reared its ugly head and I sat on the floor, rocking back and forth, trying to calm myself down.

Trapped. Totally and utterly trapped.

7

The King

In a small room aboard his ship, the King of Aureum Ignis paced back and forth, waiting for the shaking and rocking of the sea to stop.

"Can we go any faster?" he shouted to Alco, slamming his fist down on the desk as the water roared beneath him.

"We're doing all that we can, my king," Alco replied.

Storms had created a rocky journey for them on the ship, but they had no choice but to keep going. They knew it would be a long journey to find Fern, but they needed her to complete their plan.

"Alco," the king said as he walked from side to side, trying to maintain his balance, "once the storm calms, let's bring Dova back. We need to know where they went, and quickly. We can use her to find them."

He looked over at the door of the small closet that had fallen open with the movement of the ship, revealing Dova's body. It was untouched, looking just like it had before; he'd had a Potens put an enchantment on her, so she would appear the same forever, even in death.

"Yes, my king," Alco said as he hurried out of the room. "Whatever you wish." He made his way up the creaking stairs to continue studying the book with the enchantments that would be required. Although it would take more than just reading a few lines to bring her back. It might even take his soul.

The raging storm continued to wash fish up onto the deck with each wave, leaving them stranded and gasping for air. An omen, the king thought for a moment, before pushing the idea from his mind. He would make his own luck. He always had.

I waited in the cell for what felt like days, but time was hard to figure out from here. There were no windows, no sunlight, no change in the darkness. It remained dim and damp the entire time, with the slight glow of the water beneath being our only source of light. I tried to talk to the other prisoners every few hours but they never answered, just sat staring at the wall, slowly rocking back and forth. It made me anxious.

I knew that if my friends were spending their time looking for me, then they were wasting any time we had left before the king brought all of the most powerful Potens in the world back from the dead. And the longer I was in here, the less chance I had at stopping him. I was getting frustrated. I knew I was a prisoner, but I at least wanted a chance to try and reason with the queen. After all, they didn't have anything on me, and I could play dumb if I needed to.

The routine was the same every day. The guards would come in with a small bowl of food (well, I wouldn't even call it food, it was a bowl of grey mush) and I would try and talk with them, ask them how long it would take to get me out of here. But I never got an answer, they would just hand me the food and leave. I didn't give up though. Every time they came in I asked, even though they always said nothing. After a while, my stomach would be growling so loudly that it was echoing on the walls, and I'd decide to actually eat the food they gave me. I'd need to keep some sort of strength if I was going to be able to figure out a way out of here. Then, after a few hours had passed, someone else would come and pick up our empty bowls. This person looked like they might have been another of the queen's prisoners, because they had shackles on. They wouldn't talk to me either, of course. It seemed like they were all too worried about what would happen if they did.

I waited and waited for something to change. But it didn't.

Maybe I would be here forever. Maybe I would just have to accept that I was not getting out.

A door slammed open, unlike all of the other days. This was completely out of the boring routine. Three guards barged in, no food in hand.

"YOU," the lead one said, pointing in my direction, "YOUR TURN." He waved his hand, unlocking the cell.

"My turn for what?" I got to my feet, preparing for whatever came next. Even if it meant fighting until my last breath, I wouldn't give in easily. As long as I got out of this cell, I would fight until I couldn't fight any more. I knew I wasn't the strongest, but these guards didn't know what I'd been through to get here, and I wasn't going to let my story end in this place.

"You'll see soon enough," the guard said with a laugh. "Come. Out of the cell."

I took a deep breath, knowing I'd have to jump back over the water and the creatures that lay beneath. "Ok," I whispered to my-self. "Here we go." I watched the monsters swim back and forth, and took another deep breath. I had done this before, I could do it again. One, two, THREE. I leaped, landing on my knees. This time though, the creatures seemed to completely ignore my existence. Odd, I thought, as I got up and brushed the dirt off of my trousers. I wondered for a moment if, because I was being summoned by someone, they were not allowed to bite.

One of the guards grabbed my hands and put me into a pair of silver cuffs that were bound together. They were really heavy and made it hard to keep my arms up. Even when I rested my hands down, the weight of the cuffs hurt my shoulders. These were much heavier than the ones they'd had me in all those days ago, and I couldn't see myself trying to fight for my life in them. I wouldn't be able to escape the cuffs but, honestly, anything was better than dying alone in that cell. I'd thought I was starting to lose my mind down there.

Three guards surrounded me as we walked, two in the back and one in the front, guiding me toward what was sure to be a doomed end. But I couldn't lose hope now. I was out of the cell. I just had to look to what came next.

We walked back up the staircase and through the castle, passing massive hallways, what looked like old ballrooms, and even secret doors that led to new parts of the castle. I mean, this place was HUGE. I wouldn't be able to find my way back to the prison on my own even if I tried my hardest. It almost felt like they were purposely trying to confuse me. I didn't have time to ask questions, but I could have sworn that we went through a few of the rooms twice, although never in or out the same way.

All the while, I was looking around for any sort of escape. Even with the cuffs on, I would not go down without at least trying. Except, with the route they were taking me, I couldn't even plan an escape, much less pull one off, because the second I saw something that might work, we ended up back around in the same windowless room. I wasn't sure if this was happening in my head or in reality – I was sleep-deprived and hungry after all.

They eventually led me to a grand doorway, unlike all of the others. It stretched higher than any interior door I had ever seen, and we slowed our pace as we approached. I took a deep breath as the two doors creaked open, revealing red-velvet lining and shiny silver buttons that made them look quite regal.

The entrance to the queen's court was right in front of me.

I couldn't believe my eyes. This room looked nothing like any of the other rooms, and more like the outside of the building itself. It had circular architecture, and every surface was mirrored and shiny. The fact that there were no corners made the reflections in the mirrors all wonky, stretching the bodies in every direction. The design was unlike anything I had ever seen, and I couldn't stop looking around to take it all in. Honestly, the whole palace was really strange. I wasn't sure what I'd been expecting, but it was not this.

Looking at all of these mirrors, I realized that the queen must be at least a bit paranoid, because why else would you have this many mirrors? She probably used them to make sure she could see everyone at all times. After all, when you have that much power, there are always going to be people that want to try and take it from you.

I looked forward to where we were headed and there she was, sitting on a shining metal throne. The throne itself wasn't mirrored, but appeared almost muted, like she'd burned the mirrors to a faded black. She was wearing a massive dress that was completely embellished with crystals, easily the most expensive thing I had ever seen in my life. It looked like it had been dipped in red at the bottom, before fading to silver as it went up her body. The gown was tight on her waist and torso, with bare shoulders and long sleeves.

She was magnificent. And she scared me. Even from this distance.

She looked like power. And although our king was awful, the stories I'd heard about her seemed much worse. Especially with what she did to her prisoners and subjects.

We walked closer and closer, until we were about twenty feet from her. The guard directly in front of me stopped, right at the edge of the red velvet rug we had been walking on. The rug ended right before her throne, almost as if it was showing us where to stop and making sure no one got too close. Most Potens may not be able to use their gifts at this distance, but she was powerful, and I was sure she could. The thought made my heart pound a little faster.

The guard in front of me stepped to the side, putting me front and center. They all shifted, creating a barrier behind me so they could block me from leaving the room. Not that I would have been able to. The room was mirrored, there was no escape. I had been looking around for anything this whole time, a window or a door – there was nothing.

"And who is this?" the queen said.

I wasn't sure if I was supposed to speak or if she was asking the guards, so I looked back at them for a moment.

She burst into laughter. "My dear child, do you not know your own name?" she mocked.

I was confused for a moment, because if I was in a lot of trouble, wouldn't she already know who I was? Or at least why I was here?

"I do, my queen," I said as I bowed lowly to the ground, trying to show as much respect as I could. I couldn't let my ego get to me, I just needed to get out of here and fast. "I am Evergreen from the Kingdom of Aureum Ignis. I'm here visiting Jericho with... " I let my voice trail off, unsure how much of the truth I should tell. "I'm here on my own, Your Majesty," I finally said. I could feel a bead of sweat drip off of my forehead and onto the floor as I realized I may have let something slip. I didn't want her to think I was lying, but I wasn't sure what else to do. "I was just in the market, looking at the different things, when I stumbled upon a beautiful axe. It reminded me so much of one I had seen back home, and then I was taken here."

"Child, you can't lie in here," the queen said.

My heart was pounding out of my chest. How did she know I was lying?

"The mirrored walls aren't just for show," she continued. "My guard here can see frequencies in them."

She pointed to the guard that stood next to her, who I noticed was not dressed like any of the other guards. He wore a spiked helmet and all-black matte armor that looked like it would cut you if you touched it. A chill went down my spine. Maybe it was because I couldn't see what his face looked like, but he somehow looked even more intimidating than her.

"The frequencies he can see in these mirrors allow him to tell me whether you're being honest or making something up," the queen explained. "And, if I'm being honest, you want to tell me the truth on the first try. Because if you don't, well... you'll end up like the others."

She pointed to a pile of melted silver and I realized with horror that she must have turned people into the metal that was every-where here. That really grossed me out, because how many people had died for this room to be built? I had known she melted people, I had heard the stories, but I'd never thought it was possible to turn a person into metal. It didn't make sense.

I realized I would have to tell the truth. I didn't want to risk becoming melted metal, especially when my friends would never know what had happened to me. So, I mustered up the courage and took one step forward. The guards immediately grabbed the back of my shirt, to pull me back, but the queen put her hand up as if to tell them it was ok. I remained in my position and looked right at her, not wanting to show her any fear.

"I came here with friends to meet an acquaintance in Jericho. We were looking for a way to stop our king from doing something terrible. Our boat sank and we were separated. I lost all of my friends and I am eager to find them again." I could be honest without giving the entire truth to her.

"So why did you want the axe?" the queen asked.

She hadn't looked at me this entire time, but she finally shifted her gaze to meet mine and I saw that her eyes were bright orange. They looked like there was a fire burning within them. I gulped, my anxiety trying to come up. But I pushed it down – I couldn't, wouldn't, show her any fear, not now.

"I didn't want the axe as much as I wanted to see if the shopkeeper knew where my friends had gone," I said. I didn't want to tell her that the axe was a family heirloom. My grandfather's gift was famous, even here, and I couldn't let anyone know that it belonged to my family. I focused on breathing deeply between everything I said, in order to not have a major panic attack again.

The queen stood up. Her dress was even more incredible as she got to her feet. She was not very tall, and the size of the skirt looked enormous in comparison to her tiny torso. Her jet-black hair was in a slicked-back ponytail, topped with her shining metal crown. As she started coming toward me, I realized she was actually much younger than people described her. She looked no older than twenty, but I knew that couldn't be possible because she had been queen here for a century.

"I know from my sources that you have vital and valuable information that could help my kingdom get control of yours," she said, stepping so close that I could see the small fires burning in her eyes. "You see, the Kingdom of Aureum Ignis is much larger, much more vast than this one. And while I don't really care for your kingdom, I don't like the idea of someone other than me ruling it."

She paused for a moment and I wasn't sure if I should respond or not. So I waited.

"I do know where your friends are," she finally said, "and I'd be happy to send people to get them for you. But only for a trade."

My heart was racing out of my chest. My friends. "Your Majesty, how do you know that I have information that you seek?" I asked, trying to figure out how on earth she knew.

Her smile made my stomach curl. "I actually have one of your friends here. They told me everything. After many hours of pain."

My heart dropped. I couldn't live with the idea that any of them had been tortured. I couldn't even bring myself to think about whether it was Mikka or not. But I didn't want to show anger, because I knew that if I did she might not let me see them.

"So," she said matter-of-factly, "since you seem to be the key to all of this, I figured I'd give you a chance to barter. Your options here are few: you can either take the trade, or die."

"How do I know my friends are safe?" I said.

"They're not. That is why I'm offering my services to bring them here. The rest of them are currently trapped inside a cave near Jericho. It seems they went in looking for shelter, but they didn't realize the tides were turning." She smirked. "Well, they weren't turning, I just had one of my guards who's gifted in water movement block them in. They're starving, and from what I've heard from my spies, all close to death. So, I want information on the king. You give me the information, I bring your friends here."

I wondered why none of my friends had been able to use their gifts to get out of the cave, but maybe they had already been too weak when they entered. Whatever the reason, I had no choice but to make this deal. If I didn't, then we all died, and if we died, our kingdom was doomed. If we gave her the information and she tried to take the king down, our home might still be at risk, but at least if we were alive we would have a chance to save it. And while I wasn't sure living under her rule would be better than his, we could cross that bridge later. One problem at a time.

"Ok," I said, "but I want you to include in this deal that you will not harm any of my friends. Otherwise the deal is off and we're free to leave." I wasn't sure what other tricks she had up her sleeve, but I didn't want to find out.

"Deal," she said with a smirk.

The queen reached out her hand. I took it and we shook on it. I was confident that I'd just made a deal with one of the most dangerous people in the world, probably the universe, but I had to ensure the survival of my friends. And if the king successfully raised a dead army, everyone would die anyway.

The queen turned to the guard beside her, the one in all-black, and nodded. He disappeared to a hidden room behind the throne and came back out with someone I recognized.

*Helena.*

She was the one that had been captured. I couldn't imagine her ever sharing any information, and it made me realize that whatever they had done to her must have been awful. She was in bad shape, weak and exhausted. But she didn't look like she was bruised, and it made me wonder again what they'd done to her to make her talk.

Her face changed when she saw me – she was not happy to see me. "No!" she shouted. She was frightened, probably terrified that whatever they did to her, they would do to me.

"It's ok, I'm ok," I said, rushing to her. "I'm so glad to see you." I hugged her tight to prevent her from collapsing, as well as I could with the cuffs on. I'm sure I didn't look great since I'd been sitting in a wet, cold prison for days, but she looked way worse. She looked traumatized.

"I had no choice, I had to tell her," she said to me.

I shook my head. "That's ok, that's ok, I know," I said to her. I wanted to make sure she knew that I wasn't mad at her.

I couldn't imagine what kind of power the queen possessed to make Helena like this. Helena had more power than anyone I'd ever known, other than Dova. *Dova.* My mind went to that grief for a moment, but I couldn't stay there long. I looked at Helena and sighed. I felt embarrassed by what I'd just done, making a deal with the most feared queen in the world.

The queen smiled at us both. "Partners, right Evergreen?" she said.

Helena's eyes lit up as the queen confirmed what I had done. "You did not just do that," Helena said. "Please tell me you did not just make a deal with her."

I looked down at the floor. "What choice did I have? Our friends would have been left to die and it would all have been for nothing."

A tear streamed down Helena's face. I knew I had made a mistake, but it was a double-edged sword. Either I made a deal, or she let our friends die. It wasn't a hard choice. Helena would understand eventually.

The queen went back to sit on her throne, gesturing to a few of her servants. They all left and she said, "Your other friends will be here soon. Come, eat."

A table full of food appeared in front of us, unlike anything I had ever seen before. I wasn't sure if we were prisoners or partners, but I would be on my guard either way. The chains that both Helena and I were wearing shifted to become nothing more than delicate silver chain bracelets. It was a power I had seen before and Helena nodded at me, confirming that these small bracelets didn't allow you to use your gifts. That meant there was someone as powerful as Alco on the queen's side. We would have to play along for now, since Helena was nowhere near strong enough to break them.

We both ate. When we were finished, the table completely emptied and disappeared, like it had never been there at all. It made me wonder if it was just a hallucination. I hoped it was real, because I really needed the food in my system to gain my strength back. So did Helena.

The queen was reading a book on her throne. We sat patiently in silence, awaiting our friends' return.

A few hours had passed and I was beginning to feel impatient. I wanted to see Mikka.

The large doors started to shift behind us and slowly opened. In walked a large group of guards, and behind them I could see Mikka, Bondi, Gregorio and Fern. My heart wanted to leap out of my chest. They all looked even worse than Helena: they had lost weight and their lips were blue from the cold of the cave they'd been trapped in. They were very close to death.

I got out of my seat, grabbed Helena to help keep her up, and walked over to them. Bondi and Gregorio hugged me like they'd thought they would never see me again. When they grabbed Helena, they started to weep. Fern hugged me, but I was staring into Mikka's blue eyes.

"Hello," I whispered to him. I let go of Fern to hug him, wrapping my arms around him and holding tight. I hadn't been sure I was ever going to get to have this hug. "I missed you," I whispered in his ear.

"I thought you were dead," he said. "I thought you had drowned in the ocean."

"I'm here," I said. He hugged me like I was a ghost, until I finally let go of him and looked at everyone.

"How are we here?" Gregorio asked.

I knew what he really meant. We'd be dead if I hadn't made this deal.

Before I could answer though, the queen interrupted. "Let me see my group of partners."

Bondi, Gregorio and Mikka all looked at each other, very confused, as we walked over to the throne. I was holding Mikka's hand and could feel Fern's hand on my other arm.

"What an interesting bunch," the queen said as she gestured to the guards, who all immediately snapped the little chain-link bracelets on the rest of the group. "Evergreen hasn't gotten a chance to tell you yet, but you will all be helping me defeat your king so that I can take over Aureum Ignis."

Mikka looked at me with heartbreak in his eyes. "What have you done?" he said. The rest of them looked shocked and disappointed.

"Well," the queen said, "let's get started."

The queen had moved us to a large war room filled with maps and walls of books. A massive table stretched from one side of the room to the other. We all sat with our bracelets on, in silence. It had been hours since we'd all been reunited and no one had said a word.

I knew they were mad at me, but it really wasn't my fault. I'd had no choice but to make this decision for all of us. I knew that without making this deal, we would all be dead. Then who would stop the king? At least now the queen might stop him, and then maybe we could find a way to stop her.

"I'm sorry," I said out loud.

Fern looked over at me. "It's ok, I forgive you," she said.

Well, that made one person. I smiled back at her, but everyone else continued to sit in silence.

The door burst open and the queen appeared, in a new outfit. It was some kind of pantsuit, but looked like it was made of armor. Once again, I couldn't believe how young she looked in comparison to what everyone said. It was confusing, since she had to be at least a hundred but didn't look it. Not even close. She was beautiful though. Her armored pantsuit was silver, embedded with the same jet-black metal that her right-hand guard wore. The shoulders had pointed diamonds jutting out of them, large ones that few people would ever have, let alone use as a fashion statement.

"Alright, tell me what you know," she said, standing at the head of the table.

I guess we weren't going to be wasting any time on this. We all looked around at each other, not sure who would speak. I decided I would. "Well, we know he has a book that can raise the dead. We also know that he wants something or someone that can help him become immortal. We aren't sure why, or what the plan is for that." I didn't want to let slip that we knew he was after Fern. After all, we had just got her back, and I didn't want to lose anyone again. "We know that he has an extremely powerful Potens that can see into fragments of the future," I continued. "This Potens actually has multiple gifts. She's dead, but he plans to bring her back to use her powers. He might have done that already."

Dova. My grandmother.

"Who is this powerful Potens that you speak of?" the queen asked.

I looked at everyone, and Helena nodded. This was the only way we could potentially fight the king for now. "The Potens is a woman named Dova," I said.

The queen stared at me, as if she was waiting for some type of reaction, but I wasn't going to tell her that we were related. Finally she said, "Well, I have heard from my sources that he is sailing here at this very moment. I have spies everywhere, including deep within your kingdom. He won't get past the shores – my guards use their gifts to create storms out of nothing when intruders get too close. The problem is, I don't want him to go overboard or lose the ship, because then we would lose the book. And that book is what I want." She took a moment to think. "Decisions, decisions."

"Why can't you just let him land and we can take him down here?" Mikka asked.

The queen walked back and forth. "I will not let him take one step into my kingdom. I don't know what he's capable of, and without knowing who he has with him, I can't risk your king taking my land." The way she said it made it clear that there would be no possibility of that happening.

Luckily, I had another idea. "What if you let us take a boat out? Let us sail away? He would have to follow, and then you could follow all of us?"

If the king had Dova, he would see that we were making a move anyway and wouldn't get too close to the shore. It would also give us a chance to plan and escape. Mikka looked at me and smirked – I knew he'd forgive me. But I didn't want to let the queen know the plan.

"Well," she said, "it's not a bad idea, but I would join you. After all, he couldn't possibly know I was with you, could he?"

I wasn't sure how Dova's visions really worked, so I said, "I don't know, but it would be worth a shot to get him to change directions at least."

"Deal," the queen said. "Here's what we'll do."

She pulled out a massive, blank piece of paper from under the drawer at the end of the table. Once she had rolled it out, she pulled out a small dropper bottle from her suit and  applied a few drops of what looked like a shiny liquid metal onto the paper. It looked like burning metal. She put her hands just above it, not as if to touch it but to channel it in some way, and out of the small drops grew a toy-sized ship, right in front of all our eyes. It was magnificent, and if I wasn't absolutely terrified of her, I would have wanted to know how she used this gift. Her powers were both beautiful and horrifying at the same time.

"This ship is the Caretaker," the queen said. "It is the fastest, sleekest ship that we have here. It's what we'll be taking." She put her hands over the toy ship and it evolved again, spreading into the borders of the land that we were on. "This is the port we will leave from," she added, pointing to the coast of Jericho.

I looked over to see Helena's eyes light up very briefly. She quickly went back to a blank stare however, trying to hide the excitement in her eyes. I'd have to ask her later what that was all about.

"When will we leave?" I asked.

"Tonight," the queen replied. "I am having a feast shortly with a lot of the elites in town. I'll pick ten of them to join us, and then after I'm done eating and celebrating, we will leave."

Elites. I wondered if that meant the best of her guards.

Mikka sat taller in his seat. "What are you celebrating?" he asked eagerly.

"I'm celebrating my victory over your kingdom," she replied.

"Don't you think it's a bit early?" Bondi said.

Out of nowhere, Bondi was choking. I could see a small metal strand around his neck, and the queen's hands directed at him. Just as quickly, the strand disappeared.

"No, it's not," the queen said. "The victory is mine." With that, she stormed out of the room, taking her guards with her and locking the door behind her.

"Bondi, are you ok?" I said as I rushed over to him.

"I'm fine, I'm fine," he replied, rubbing his neck.

"What the heck is her problem?" Mikka asked.

"I don't know," I said, and then turned to Helena, hoping no one was listening in on us. "Helena, what was that look about earlier?"

She looked around, checking it was just us in the room before speaking. "Well, we came here to get some help from a friend of mine. Her name is Kilko. She lives in Jericho, in the town. If she sees a parade with the queen and us headed to port, she'll find a way to join us. I won't say more now."

Hope. There was hope after all.

The guards left us, and we spent the evening whispering about what we could do if Kilko got on board with us. We discussed what the plan would be if we needed to escape on the water, and what to do if the queen did get the Book of Viempro. We went over every scenario but none were perfect, which made this entire planning thing kind of pointless. In fact, every plan we came up with seemed doomed to end in some sort of disaster, but any situation was better than the one we were in now, because at least it was a step closer to stopping the king.

While everyone was talking, I moved my chair closer to Mikka's. "I missed you so much," I said as I placed my hand in his. "I was worried sick about you."

"Me too," he said as he held my hand a little tighter. "Me too."

"What can Kilko do?" I heard Fern say to Helena.

"I don't want to speak of it yet, she'll show you when we see her," Helena replied.

"How will she know you're here?" I asked, wondering how Kilko could possibly know that we were on this island, let alone that we needed her help.

Helena smiled. "She knows... everything."

I wondered for a moment if that meant she had a gift similar to Dova's. I also wondered for a moment if the queen had heard our entire conversation, but at this point it didn't matter. She was forcing us into this partnership anyway and she had to know that we weren't happy with the deal.

The doors suddenly burst open, revealing the queen in yet in another outfit. It was another suit, but red, sparkling with small, mirror-like crystals all over. The reflections in each of the crystals made it both difficult to look at and hard to look away.

"Alright partners, let's get going." The queen spoke as if we were all good friends. "We only have a short window to lure the king out to sea before they crash on the shores."

I knew we couldn't trust her, but she was certainly trying to make it seem like we should. I wouldn't let my guard down, though. You had to treat everyone like they were out for blood, because they were.

Still stuck with our gift-controlling bracelets, we walked with the queen and her guards, including the terrifying one in all-black triple-pointed armor. The pace was exhausting, all of us were struggling just trying to keep up with them. We knew we'd need as much strength as possible if we were going to attack the king, but we had no choice but to hurry after the group. They led us out of the winding, ridiculously confusing castle to a row of carriages outside which took us down a rocky road. We were being bumped about for almost the entire journey, and I felt like I would be sick.

Mikka, Fern, the queen and myself were in one carriage, while the jet-black armored guard was in the other with Bondi, Gregorio and Helena. None of us were able to use our gifts so it didn't really matter that we were separated – we were all in a bad spot. I wanted to get out of there so desperately that I spent the ride staring out of the small window of the carriage, trying to see if I could see the shore.

"Sick?" the queen said to me.

"Yes, Your Majesty," I said back.

She let out a belly laugh that startled both me and Fern. Fern grabbed Mikka's hand a bit tighter as the queen said, "Girl, you do not need to address me so properly. "You can call me Emmeria." She seemed as terrifying as people made her out to be, but I wanted to know what had changed her into the monster she was described as, so I nodded. She looked out of the window and continued, "Go ahead and ask. I know you've been wondering it."

"Wondering what?" I asked. I had so many questions.

"Wondering how I look like this, considering my age," she said, turning her gaze back to me.

"Oh," I said. "Umm, yeah, I have been wondering that. I heard that you were over a hundred. How is that possible when you look like you're only twenty?" Mikka looked at me with a shocked expression – he must not have heard the tales about the queen being far older than the woman in front us.

The queen, Emmeria, sat up in her seat. She was beautiful. And terrifying. "I know you are all aware that one of my gifts is the ability to melt and meld metal," she said, "but what most people don't know is that I have even more gifts than anyone knows. There is no time for the full story, however, and that is all I'll reveal for now."

That statement left me with more questions than answers. Dova had made it seem like being an Untouchable was unheard of, so I'd thought that there weren't many Potens out there with more than one gift. But Emmeria must have been one too. Her ability to shift metal alone was incredible, but if she had other gifts then she was even more powerful than we had guessed.

I wanted to know what gift she was talking about, that made her look younger, but I was afraid to ask another question. I already felt like we were walking on thin ice with her, and I knew what she had done to people. It really did make me hate her. Instead, I peeked outside through the small curtain as we continued our journey. The carriages went by so many different landscapes, a lot of which I'd seen on my way in and some that were completely new. We finally pulled up to the coast of Jericho, where the road felt a little smoother, as if the path was paved.

"We're here," Emmeria said.

I was shocked to see the small town of Jericho. It was much more rustic than I'd anticipated and seemed tiny compared to the massive city we had just come from. It didn't have that futuristic feel that the queen's castle had, there was instead a lot of peeling paint and old wood on these homes.

Looking at out them, I felt anxious. Not my normal form of panic attack, just generally worried that things were going to go wrong. We needed Helena's friend to find us, but I wasn't sure how easy that would be. I also wasn't sure what would be worse after we found the king: having the king in power, or the queen. Both options were awful.

The carriage came to a halt and Emmeria stood up. I didn't dare stand up until after she was out of the carriage; I couldn't risk what might happen if I made her mad. I was playing it safe, we all were right now. The door opened swiftly from the outside and the queen stepped gracefully out. Mikka and I went next, and I reached back to grab little Fern. As I pulled her from the carriage, I worried about the part she might play in all of this. About what she may need to do to stop all of this madness. I pushed that thought to the side though. There was no time for it right now.

Outside of the carriage was a dock holding a massive ship, unlike anything I had ever seen before. There were tons of guards, all in armor, loading up the vessel. There were way more than I had anticipated. Emmeria had said she was bringing ten elites, but this was more like thirty. It wasn't going to be easy to find a way to escape with this many eyes on us.

I saw Helena, Gregorio and Bondi step out of the other carriage, and we were all instructed to hurry toward to ship. Emmeria didn't seem like she would be waiting for anyone. She wanted what the king had, and badly. She also wanted it fast. So I picked up my pace, trying to hurry Fern along.

"This way," a guard shouted at us.

We followed. There would be a time to disobey, to destroy all that was theirs, but now was not that time. Now, we needed to prepare for what was to come, so we let ourselves be pushed down into the lower deck of the ship and into a cell. Great. Another prison, this one on the sea. I didn't want to be confined to yet another cell, especially one where I was going to get seasick.

We all looked around at one another, as if waiting for a sign that Kilko was on board. I kept staring at Helena but didn't dare speak of it because I wasn't sure what anyone's gifts were. Instead, we all stood in silence, listening as the large groups of guards boarded the ship with massive amounts of weapons. We waited and waited and waited, for any sign from Helena that she'd seen Kilko, but she just stood still, staring out of the bars of the tiny, gated chamber that we were in. Guards passed back and forth, moving things as they hurried to leave the port.

The boat shifted suddenly, knocking all of us off balance and off of our feet onto the floor. We were moving. My heart started pounding. I didn't want to see the king. Not now, not this soon. I looked at Fern, knowing that the king would do anything to get to her. Without saying anything, I just put my hand on her shoulder. I would not let that happen.

But even though I tried to focus on that thought, it felt like the earth had gone out from under my feet. Sea sickness, again. I couldn't seem to kick it, no matter how hard I tried. Letting go of Fern's shoulder, I tried to ease my swaying from side to side by holding the bars of the cell tightly. But the waves kept coming. Not being able to see the horizon made it so much worse.

Mikka put his hand on my back, trying to comfort me. It was a little helpful, just knowing that everyone was here for me, but I felt like I would be useless in a fight on the water given how sick I was feeling. Bondi and Gregorio were looking around anxiously, and I thought about how helpful it would be if Gregorio could shift. But we were still under the spell of Emmeria's bracelets, making them more like chains. We were trapped here, headed toward the king.

I took a deep breath and sat. A tear ran down my face. We had to find a way out. We had to hold out hope.

# 11

The constant rocking wouldn't stop. I felt like I would throw up at any moment, which was inconvenient because I needed to be at my best when we fought the king.

Helena was pacing around frantically. She was still waiting for any sign of Kilko but we'd seen nothing yet and it had to have been a few hours since we left the dock. I knew if Kilko hadn't boarded the ship then any chance of a surprise escape would be gone.

Hope was the only thing we could do in this situation, the only way to keep moving forward, no matter how hard. Hope that one miracle would lead to another and we would find a way out of this disaster.

Mikka sat quietly with Fern, holding her hand. He was trying to reassure her that everything would be alright but the truth was, even though she was little, she had seen so much already. I think she was a little numb to it all now. She sat there with a blank expression, like it was all just another regular day for her. I couldn't imagine what it must have been like for her to sit in the castle while she knew her mother had died. She wasn't the only one, we had all been through too much but we couldn't stop now. I shook my head, trying to let go of the stress of everything around us. I needed to focus but the stress and the grumble of my stomach made it hard to.

A loud noise sounded from above us, like something crashing down onto the ceiling. For a moment after there was loud shouting from above, and then everything went quiet. Complete and utter silence.

"What was that?" Bondi said, looking around to see if he could figure out what it was.

"I'm not quite sure," Helena said as she moved closer to the bars of the cell.

We could hear the waves crashing against the sides of the ship, and I could hear my heartbeat racing as my mind started to wonder what had happened to everyone on the boat. Loud footsteps started to echo above and the door to the chamber we were in opened abruptly. Someone was heading swiftly down the stairs, dressed in a Queen's Guard uniform. They took a step closer and started shedding their uniform, piece by piece. The woman underneath was dressed in a head-to-toe matte-black outfit; from under the helmet appeared long, beautiful blonde curls that went past her hips. She had piercing blue eyes, with tiny freckles on her nose and underneath her eyes that framed her face nicely.

"Long time no see," she said aloud.

This must be Kilko. We were saved. Hope always wins.

Helena smirked at her and said, "It's good to see you." They grabbed each other's hands through the bars of the cell and embraced one another as best they could. "This is Kilko," Helena told us with a big smile as she gestured towards her friend.

We all smiled and nodded, now knowing we were getting out of here alive. Kilko had the keys to our cages on her belt, so she reached down and opened them for us to get out.

"Where's Emmeria?" I said quietly, afraid she would appear from the open door above.

"She's sleeping," Kilko said. "We don't have much time."

"Sleeping? Like she's taking a nap?" I asked, confused.

"Yeah, sort of. We have to hurry, everyone will be up soon."

"Everyone?" I said. "What do you mean, everyone's sleeping? Where are we going to go? We're on the ocean."

Kilko smiled. "We have a small boat, the emergency boat for this one. It will fit us all if we squeeze together. I'll take you back to your kingdom."

My eyes filled with happy tears. We were getting out of here. Kilko used another key to take off the bracelets that were stopping us from using our gifts. It felt like a breath of fresh air to get those things off. Looking down at the bracelet, I thought about how similar this type of power was to Alco's. Even though he couldn't be working for her, Emmeria had to have a lot of powerful Potens connections – this was difficult magic.

We hurried along up the steps and to the top of the boat. The small lifeboat was already floating alongside our larger ship; Kilko must have prepared it before coming down to get us. All of the guards were laying down, some of them snoring, and I was certain that it was because of Kilko's gift. That must be one of the coolest gifts ever, to just be able to put people to sleep. I was sure she'd used it a lot to escape when needed. All I could do was make tea... but I guess it has saved us before.

We hurried onto the lifeboat, although I didn't see how this would help us when everyone woke up. After all, the queen had claimed hers was the fastest ship in the kingdom. We also needed to stop the king from getting to the queen before one of them killed the other for that book, a book that we needed to steal back.

As Kilko and Bondi took the ropes off of the lifeboat to

disconnect us from the ship, I asked worriedly, "How long will they sleep for?"

Kilko didn't look up at me, just shook her head as she continued trying to untie the ropes. "Not long," she said quickly.

Kilko pushed us off the main boat and we started to paddle away, Gregorio creating winds to move us a bit faster. We weren't going as fast as the ship would be, but at least we were moving faster than I'd expected. Gregorio was shoving us on, and I could see another boat in the distance now, although I couldn't quite make out the emblem on their flag.

Emmeria screamed as she awoke from her slumber. I could hear it even from here as her voice carried over the water. "GET THEM!"

The waves suddenly started getting bigger, way too big for this tiny lifeboat that could barely fit all of us. The clouds rolled in and massive strikes of lightning started to shimmer around us. I knew it had to be a Potens creating this kind of storm, but it wasn't anyone on our boat. Meanwhile, the boat in the distance was getting closer. I squinted, and finally recognized the king's emblem.

We now had two very big problems. One, we were going to be intercepted by the king, and two, our small lifeboat was taking on water, getting higher by the minute and starting to cover our ankles.

"Mikka, what do we do?!" I shouted through the torrential rain and cracks of lightning that swirled around us.

I looked, panicked, at the rest of our group. It was in moments like these where I wished I had more power than just being a tea maker.

"We need to make it to that other boat, even if it is the king," Mikka said with defeat in his voice.

He was right. It was better to run toward the king and at least have someone to try and fight Emmeria off than it was to stay in our small sinking boat in this Potens-caused weather. But although I knew he was right, it would not make things easier. We could either go back to the queen's boat where I was certain she would kill one of us for leaving, or we could head to the king's boat where Fern would most certainly be taken captive.

"Kilko, how far does your gift work?" I asked, looking at her with my eyes filled with hope.

"Unfortunately, not that far," she shouted as Gregorio's gift moved us in the direction of the king's boat. "I have to be within a few feet of them for it to work."

The waves were getting more and more violent with each passing minute, and had gotten so big that we almost capsized a few times. The storm was raging more wildly, and the roar of the wind made everything so hard to hear. The air was suddenly cold. On top of us all being absolutely soaked from the rain, the waves were now freezing as they hit our ship, leaving icicles onboard.

It was unbearable, sitting in this sinking ship. This was not how we were going to die.

"Kilko, I have an idea," I shouted as my teeth chattered and my stomach turned. She looked over at me, everyone else leaning in to hear me. "Who's the best swimmer?" I yelled. Bondi raised his hand and I nodded in agreement. "Kilko and Bondi, jump off and swim together towards the king's boat. Get just close enough that you can put them all to sleep and then bring the boat our way."

Everyone looked at me, understanding that this was probably our only option. Or at least our only option that would lead us to some sort of safety. The queen's boat was heading our way and we were running out of time.

Kilko nodded. "I'll raise the flag once we're on so you know it's safe and then you can all get closer," she said.

"Are you sure this is a good idea?" Gregorio asked. "They might freeze to death before they even get there," he added, worried for his brother.

"No, I'm not sure, but we have to do something," I shouted over the wind as the freezing waves and chilling gusts ripped through the air.

I knew he was right. It was dangerous to send them into the water, especially in this storm. But I hoped that the Potens creating it would keep the storm around our boat and that they would have an easier time swimming.

"Then it sounds like a plan," Gregorio said.

Kilko and Bondi looked at one another and jumped off in unison, swimming as hard as they could toward King Jett's boat. They kept heading in that direction even as the waves crashed upon them. I couldn't understand how they would be able to keep going through this storm, but we had to try it. I knew for certain that what they were doing was dangerous, but I also knew it was necessary. We would die out here if we didn't find some way to get help.

As Kilko and Bondi swam closer to the king's ship, it did look like the waves got smaller around them, so we all sat, bearing with the storm and waiting to see if they would make it. Mikka was holding Fern tightly to try and keep her warm during this disaster, which was almost impossible. The rain was coming in sideways and the water we'd been taking on was well above our ankles now. We didn't have much time left. Gregorio was trying to whisk the water off of the boat with his gift, but the actual wind around us was too strong.

Looking behind us, I saw Emmeria standing at the front of her ship, staring at us. I knew she felt betrayed. I also knew that she could melt us from this distance. She was closer than I was comfortable with, but we didn't have a lot of options to get away right now. I grabbed Gregorio's arm to show him where she was standing and shouted, "Gregorio, transform into wind to push us farther away, I think she's going to try and hurt us!"

"I can't, I have no more energy!" Gregorio desperately needed to rest after having pushed us out this far; he'd spent the last of his energy trying to get the water out of the boat.

As the queen continued to watch us from her ship, the waves around us got bigger and bigger. I couldn't see much from here, but I could see that she was smiling. My heart dropped as I watched the queen raise her arms up and point them towards us. I closed my eyes, and for a moment I wondered if it would be quick. I could only hope that it would be a fast death.

But nothing happened.

When I opened my eyes, Emmeria wasn't standing at the front of the ship anymore. She must have gone below. I wondered why, but was thankful that none of us were a pile of metal. Looking around, I couldn't see Bondi or Kilko anymore––they must have made it to the king's ship––but I could see Helena. She was standing up on our boat, even in the wind and freezing rain. That was why the queen had hid: Helena was looking directly at the ship, her eyes glowing red and as she smiled from ear to ear.

Helena stepped up onto the small seat of the lifeboat. She was making us unbalanced but it didn't matter, we were going to sink anyway. Helena put her hands out, her palms facing the queen's ship. The guards that were standing on the edge of the vessel were looking in our direction, getting ready to use their gifts, but it was too late for them. Helena started to shake and all of the guards fell down. They weren't sleeping though. They would never wake back up. Mikka covered Fern's eyes.

Helena fell over and I grabbed her. "You ok?" I asked.

She brushed me off. "I'm fine, just need a moment," she said, sitting down in the pool of water in our small boat and closing her eyes. When she opened them, they were back to normal.

The rain stopped abruptly and the sky cleared. One of the Potens Helena had just killed must have been the one causing the storm. I used my hands to make a cup and starting throwing the water off of the boat, getting as much of it out as possible. The sun came out too and instantly started to warm us all up. Thank the heavens, because I wasn't sure how much more of that cold I could've taken.

"They made it," Mikka said quietly.

The king's flag was raised high and the boat was headed our way.

Hope. There was hope once again.

We paddled over as fast as we could, hoping that Helena had also managed to take out Emmeria, since we couldn't hear anyone on the queen's ship and the weather was still calm. But I kept looking over at Emmeria's boat anyway. Something just felt off. Meanwhile, the king's shining, golden-trimmed boat pulled up alongside us and someone threw down a rope ladder. We had Fern go up first, then Mikka, then Helena, then Gregorio, then me. I pulled myself up onto the deck.

"Well, isn't it nice to see you again."

King Jett stepped calmly out of the shadows of the boat. He was holding Fern's hand, while the rest of my friends each had a guard at their back. Bondi and Kilko were nowhere to be seen.

It was a trap.

# 12

Part of me was horribly angry at myself for allowing us to walk into this again. The other part of me was thankful that we were out of that storm and on a larger ship now. My friends had been restrained by a glowing circular ring, and I didn't know how we would escape.

"You must be so foolish," King Jett said, "to have thought that you could just walk onto my ship and take what is rightfully mine." He stepped closer, pulling Fern along behind him. "You all have no powers in that circle," the king went on, "and no way of getting out of here this time. And Bondi and Kilko, well, they're in the same situation. And I don't even need to put you in that circle, Evergreen, you're practically powerless after all." He laughed.

I looked around for Alco but I couldn't see him yet. I didn't know where Bondi and Kilko were either, which worried me. But when I looked over at Helena, I noticed that her eyes were turning red. She stepped slightly out of the circle, though not enough for anyone to notice. The glowing ring somehow hadn't worked on her and she flashed her eyes back to normal, so that only I had seen it.

Helena could get us out of here. I knew she was exhausted from just using her gift on the queen's ship, so we would have to wait for her energy to come back before choosing the perfect moment to strike.

"Where are Bondi and Kilko?" I asked the king, realizing that we had to buy enough time to find our friends and make sure they were ok. Then Helena would be our element of surprise.

"You'll see soon enough," the king replied. "All I need now is to get rid of the rest of you."

As King Jett spoke, Alco came out from beneath the shadows of the ship, holding the Book of Viempro in one hand. I glanced very quickly at Helena. We would have to find a way to take it from them, before anyone was able to use the book against us. Helena was waiting for the perfect moment to attack, so I said again, firmly, "Where are Bondi and Kilko?"

The king let out a low laugh. "Like I said, you'll see soon enough."

The guards started to shove us towards the bow of the ship, pushing us up the small flight of stairs and onto the top deck where I could see both Kilko and Bondi. They both had heavy chains tied to their feet, with massive weights on the bottom. They too were in a small, floating ring that was preventing Kilko from using her gift. They were also very close to the edge of the deck.

I realized what was coming. There were two guards ready to shove them into the water, and with the weights on their feet, they would not be able to come back up.

I had to buy us more time, so I shouted, "Wait! There's something you're not understanding about all of this." My voice was shaking, but I took a step closer to Alco.

Alco, who had the book in his hand, let out a laugh. "Tea maker, what are you going to do?" He smiled through the question.

"Ever, what are you doing?" Mikka asked with confusion. He

hadn't seen that Helena was somehow not affected by that ring. I looked at him for a moment, but I couldn't give anything away.

The king took a step forward, grabbing Fern's wrist tightly as if he was afraid she would get out of his sight. "What do you think I don't understand?" he said angrily.

I smiled, realizing he was actually afraid that he was missing something. I paced around for a moment, to buy us just a little more time and allow Helena to regain just a little more energy. I looked over at her and she flashed her eyes red at me, letting me know she was ready.

"What you don't understand," I told the king, "is that you think you're smarter than us, but in fact, you're not." And then I shouted, "NOW!"

Helena used the rest of her energy to break the rings that were preventing the Potens from using their gifts, but the guards next to Kilko and Bondi shoved them overboard before any of us could stop them. Thankfully, as Kilko fell into the water, she reached up to put everyone on the boat to sleep with her power. We didn't have much time though, they wouldn't stay asleep for long.

The king dropped to the ground and Fern fell with him for just a moment. She peeled his fingers off her arm, got up and ran over to us. Gregorio dove off the boat, quickly transforming into air to move faster toward Bondi and Kilko as they sank deeper and deeper into the ocean. I couldn't see what Gregorio was doing from up here, but I knew he had to catch up to them and break their chains. We all stood watching the water, waiting for a sign of any of them to come back up, but there was nothing. I was holding my breath in anticipation.

Moments later, Gregorio, Bondi and Kilko's heads burst through the surface of the ocean waves, gasping for air. Bondi was choking on the water, but he was ok. Mikka and I pulled them on board.

"How did you know?" Mikka said to me as he pulled Gregorio up.

"Helena's eyes were glowing red when I came onboard," I said as I pulled Kilko up. "Somehow it wasn't working on her. I just knew I needed to buy us a little time."

Once Bondi, Gregorio and Kilko were back onboard, Mikka walked over and gave me a big hug. "You saved us," he said.

"No, Helena did," I said, looking over his shoulder at Helena. She smiled at me.

We all started throwing the guards, the king and Alco off of the boat, but not before we grabbed the Book of Viempro. I ran downstairs to see if anyone else was onboard, opened one of the doors, and there was Dova.

My heart sank and I fell to the floor. She somehow looked the same as she had when she was alive: beautiful and wrinkled. I could hear commotion overhead though, so I closed the door and ran back up the stairs. Kilko was looking over the edge at the floating bodies of the guards, the king and Alco. Gregorio and Bondi were finishing preparing the ship, and Mikka had started steering us in the direction of our home kingdom.

Gregorio was exhausted but we needed his gift more than ever right now. So, with the small amount of energy he had left, he pushed us faster with the wind. As we sailed out to sea, I looked back at the queen's boat to see all the Kingsmen, the king and Alco boarding her boat. It looked like one of the living queen's guards awoke them and saved them from drowning. I'd hoped that Helena had killed the queen earlier, but something in my gut told me she was still alive.

The thought of them working together was much scarier than just facing one of them. We couldn't worry about that now, though. Onward.

Hours must have gone by as we sailed in silence. There was no sight of the other ship anymore. We had the book, Fern and all our friends on this boat, but it didn't feel like a victory. I knew there would be much more to come before we could rest. But, for now, we had to enjoy this moment because we didn't know how many of these moments we would have left.

Bondi was getting a pyre ready. Earlier, I had mentioned that if we found Dova we should give her the proper send-off, one that that would prevent anybody from using her gifts after death. So Bondi had spent all afternoon gathering material that we could burn and placing it in the small wooden lifeboat that was on the king's ship. Once the materials were ready, we carefully assembled the pyre so that it would burn properly. Gregorio, Bondi, Helena and I carried Dova's lifeless body and placed it on top of the pyre. The moonlight shone above and the stars twinkled as we all sat around the small funeral boat.

"I'd like to say something before we send her off," I said. "Dova, although I didn't know you for very long, I do know that you were family. I thank you for the bravery that you showed me I had, the connection I had to you and Grandpa, and for being as fierce as you were, up until the very end." I laid a flower that I'd found on her body.

Everyone else shared a few words, and then we lit the pyre and sent it out to sea in the lifeboat. It was engulfed by flames, giving Dova the final rest that she deserved. Now, no one would be able to use her gifts. She would be able to finally be at peace.

Bondi, Gregorio and Helena comforted one another. They had spent so much time in the Zirkels with Dova that I knew this had to be hard for them. Mikka held me as a tear streamed down my face.

I didn't have much left in me, but Dova had been my grandmother. She would always have a place in my heart. I sat with Mikka on one side and Fern on the other, both of them comforting me as the small boat slowly burned in the distance until it sank into the depths of the ocean.

We took turns taking watch, deciding on an order of who would stay up and when others would be allowed time to rest. I didn't know what was going to come, and I had so many questions for Kilko, but they would have to wait until the morning.

I stared at the stars above as I thought about everything that had happened so far. I couldn't quite wrap my head around the fact that it seemed like everyone was just hungry for power. It felt like no matter how hard we tried, there would still be someone who wanted to use the Book of Viempro and its powers. If we did find a way to stop all of this, we would have to find a long-term solution for the kingdom, because just allowing another power-hungry person to step onto the throne would cause even more problems.

We'd decided earlier that whoever stayed up would sit with the book, to protect it from anyone who might sneak up on us. When it was my turn to stay up and guard the book, I kissed Mikka on his forehead as he slept and got up to trade shifts with Helena. She nodded at me as she saw me get up, knowing that she could rest now. I grabbed the book and sat there under the moonlight with it in my hands, wondering why I couldn't just rip it up or destroy it. I wanted to wake Kilko and ask her, or Helena even, but I needed to let them sleep. We would have time for questions in the morning.

I started flipping through the pages of the book to see what was written on them, but it all was in a text that I didn't understand.

I knew I should have paid more attention to the languages classes that I'd sat through in school.

Never mind that though, there wasn't time to sit here and judge myself about what I hadn't done right. I never would have thought I'd have the courage to do half of the things I'd done up to this point, and for that I needed to be proud of myself and less judgmental.

I took a deep breath, closed the book and looked back up at the stars above me. They were bright and beautiful on the cloudless night that it turned out to be. I wondered if I would ever have a home one day, with family, where I could sit out on my porch and do this every night. Maybe in a different life, maybe if I was a different person. I had to hold on to that hope that things might be different, *could* be different, if we were able to defeat the evil that was in our realm.

Maybe we should have killed the king back there. But that would have made us just like him.

An hour passed by and my racing thoughts were interrupted by a soft voice from behind me.

"Ever, it's your turn," Bondi said.

I could go back to sleep. We'd decided to take short shifts, since we wouldn't have too much darkness left for rest. I nodded and quietly passed the book off to Bondi before laying down on the wooden floor with one of the small blankets that we'd found below deck. I closed my eyes, trying to shut out the dangers of what was to come, and drifted off to sleep.

# 13

I awoke to the laughter of my friends on the ship.

*My friends.*

I knew that having close relationships was dangerous, because the second you start to love someone or something, it becomes hard to lose. But I loved having this group of people now that felt like family.

"Good morning," Mikka said, leaning over and kissing me on the cheek.

"Good morning," I said back with a smile.

Before getting up and walking over to where everyone else was sitting, I gave Fern a hug. She was quiet and never said much, but I knew she was happy to be here with all of us. Everyone else was sitting in a circle near the steering wheel of the ship so that Helena could steer but also be a part of the conversation. Gregorio was passing out some sort of porridge that he'd made from what he'd found in the kitchen, and I grabbed a small bowl. The warm porridge was so nice to eat in the chill of the morning and we spent our time laughing at the bad jokes that Bondi was telling. He was trying to get our minds off of everything, even if it was just for a little while. When we had all finished our porridge, we sat in silence for a moment, thinking about what would be next.

"Kilko, I do have some questions that maybe you could answer," I said as I cleaned the bowl with my spoon, thankful for some warm food. Helena was just a few steps away from our circle, holding on to the wheel of the ship to make sure we were headed in the right direction. She looked over at me as I spoke and then at Kilko, waiting to see what her reply would be.

"Yes, I have some as well, but you can go first," Kilko said as she started to collect everyone's empty porridge bowls and stack them on the ground for now.

"Well, for starters, where are we going to go?" I said, not just to Kilko but to the group. Everyone was looking at Kilko though, also wondering that same thought.

"We're headed back to Aureum Ignis. I know a place where we would be safe there," she said.

"How do you know somewhere to go that's in a different kingdom?" Mikka interrupted. Kilko lived in Melted Cor, so it was strange that she would have an idea of where to go in Aureum Ignis.

"Well, what has Helena told you of me?" Kilko asked as she looked over at Helena.

"Honestly, not much," Bondi said. "She did mention that you somehow know everything, but other than that she didn't tell us much because she didn't want the queen or her guards hearing." We all looked at Kilko and noticed that Helena was looking at her lovingly. They seemed to be very good friends that had been apart for a long time.

Kilko laughed. "Well, Helena, you gave me more credit than I deserve," she said, continuing to laugh. She cleared her throat. "I mean, I don't know everything. Like, it's not a gift anyway. My gift is, as you saw, that I can bring hundreds to sleep at once, within a short range. It's proved to be a very helpful gift over the past years when I've been constantly running from one place to another. Jericho is my home, but I've traveled pretty much everywhere." She looked at Helena and smiled. "The reason Helena said I know everything is because, well, I've done a lot of favors for people over the years, and I mean A LOT. I've helped out some of the most important people you have and haven't heard of. And I hate to admit this, but I've even helped out the queen." None of us made a sound, trying to listen to her every word.

"With these favors I've traded information, and at this point I've traded so much information that there isn't a boat docking in Jericho that I don't already know who and what valuable information or resources are on it." She said it proudly, and my eyebrows were raised as I waited for her to continue. "I'd heard what was happening in your kingdom, I'd heard what had happened to Dova, I'd heard whispers that you were all headed my way. Helena and I were friends when we were both young, we bonded over the severity of our gifts, so I knew I had to help."

I felt massive relief. We were lucky to have Kilko join our group. We needed her for whatever would be next. I also felt like I could trust her, because if Helena could trust her, that meant we all could.

"Ok, well, when we get to this place, what then?" I said sternly, looking over at the book on the floor. "Can't we just burn the book and let them cut their losses with it? It's not like we need it."

"Unfortunately, the book has some kind of curse," Kilko explained. "We can't get rid of it. If you do burn it, it reappears somewhere else in the world. And while that could be helpful in the moment, we wouldn't know where it would reappear. Also, with the kind of power the book possesses, we can't take the chance of it falling into the wrong hands. We have to find a way to hide it, like it was for years before."

I couldn't think of a single safe place to hide it, but we would deal with that later. I looked at both Mikka and Fern. "What do you know about Fern?"

Kilko's expression went from confident to solemn, which gave me the chills. Her expression made me think that this was not a good thing to be asking in front of Fern, so I quickly said, "Maybe we should have Fern go below deck with someone."

"Nnnnn... nnno. I want to hear. If it's about me, I want to know," Fern said with a shaky voice.

Mikka nodded. "She's going to have to learn at some point, and after everything she's already been through, it wouldn't hurt for her to know the truth," he said as he looked at his sister.

I knew he was right, but she was still so young that it was hard not to want to shelter her from something that might be awful to hear. But it was truly up to Mikka. Kilko paused for a moment to let the silence linger, until Mikka nodded at her to show that he was ok with her continuing. Kilko looked down as if she was unsure about telling us what came next. Finally, she looked back up at Fern with a little smile, and then looked at me to answer my question.

"Well, what I've heard was that there was a little girl who not too long ago was given this gift of eternal life by a Tree Witch. I didn't know who the girl was, but now that I do, it all makes sense. I didn't know it was Fern until I met her."

"Wait, how did you know it was her?" Mikka interrupted.

Kilko smiled and said, "She has gifts that I can sense. I don't know what kind, but it's a strong, abnormal amount of power. I'm sure that's why Alco wanted to help the king too. There's some sort of energy you can feel when you look at Fern, one that just makes you want to see the potential of her gifts."

"Well, how come none of us knew?" Mikka asked.

Kilko paused for a moment. "I think you probably all felt something, it's just that you weren't fully in-tune with what that something meant."

Mikka looked puzzled. I hadn't felt anything that made me think Fern was different, but we also hadn't been paying attention to that.

Kilko continued. "Long ago, there was a story about something that would happen in the future. It seems like the story was about Fern. The story told that a girl would be given gifts by a powerful witch, and that she would be the one to stop the darkness from growing. But if she didn't, the darkness would... " Kilko paused.

"The darkness would what?" Mikka said sternly, demanding to know what was next.

Kilko looked over at Fern and said, "The darkness would become her."

"What does this mean?" I asked.

Kilko gulped. "It means that either Fern is the one who can stop the darkness, which in our case is the king and queen both trying to bring the dead back to life to use their gifts, or she'll become the darkest type of gift, one that will destroy us all."

"But Fern's never shown any powers," Mikka said, frightened that the story could be true.

"Well, we don't know for sure," I said. After everything we had been through, who could really know if Fern had more gifts then we knew, even if Kilko said she could feel it.

"It's a story from long ago, so it doesn't mean it's going to be fully true," Kilko said, trying to reassure Mikka that there was the possibility of a different option for the future. "All I know is the story, so I'm sharing it with all of you. When I heard that there was a girl who had become immortal because of a Tree Witch, I knew it had to be the same story. But stories can change."

"How do we stop this from happening?" I asked Kilko.

"Well, I believe that there is a way for Fern to transfer the bond of immortality, but it's permanent and rare. If she did, she couldn't ever get it back. And right now, Fern will live forever, so why would she want to give that away." Kilko didn't say it as a question.

"I don't want it," Fern said, scared. "I want to give it away."

"I think for now, love, you just keep it and we can talk about that at a later time. Right now it's about keeping you safe from harm," Mikka said.

He was both right and wrong. Sure, the gift was preventing her from dying, but it was also one of the main reasons the king was after us.

"That's why the king wants her," I said under my breath as I realized what he'd been trying to do all along. "He wants to take her immortality." Then I said, aloud, "One other thing, Kilko. The queen––"

Kilko quickly interrupted me. "I knew you were going to ask about her. I know she looks, what, twenty? And she's supposed to be over a hundred. It is crazy, but it isn't immortality. I don't know how to explain it because I don't quite understand it myself, but I don't think she's the real queen."

"What? What do you mean she's not the queen?" I said in disbelief. Everyone around me looked equally puzzled, and even Helena looked over in confusion.

"I met the queen years ago and she was old, even then," Kilko explained. "But when I went to meet her again, she looked like she does now. I challenged her on it, asked her about something we had talked about a few years before. She acted like she remembered, which was so odd, considering she looked completely different. The guard in black and this 'queen' just showed up one day and something suspicious has been going on ever since."

"I'm confused," I said, feeling sick. "You don't think she's the actual queen? Then how do you explain that she has the same gift?" How could this be possible? I knew the stories, but I didn't think anyone could fake being the queen. After all, how would she have taken over her palace? How would she have convinced the entire kingdom?

"I don't know how's she's doing it," Kilko said, shrugging. "It could be the same person, sure, but I just have a feeling that it's not."

We all sat looking at one another. I was trying to piece every-thing together but none of it really made any sense. What did make sense though was that the queen rarely made herself visible to the people outside of her castle, so maybe they wouldn't have noticed the change. But I couldn't quite wrap my head around all of it, I still needed to know more.

"Do you have any proof of this?" I asked Kilko.

"Just what I've told you," she said. "But there have been tons of whispers about it throughout the kingdom. It's just that any time someone voices it, they disappear or die."

Something was off about all of this. I knew that if people were disappearing or dying just for speaking their minds on the issue that there had to be something of truth in there. I took a deep breath as I looked over the edge of the ship.

"Shore," Helena said aloud.

We'd made it back to our kingdom. Thank the heavens.

We were on a completely different side of Aureum Ignis. I had never been this far north. That seemed to be the way lately, always moving in a new direction, something I hadn't experienced before. I had liked my comfortable tea shop in Kinver, I had liked being able to go into the woods and climb and backpack. I had liked the comfort of being close to home. This was all a shock to the system.

As we got closer to shore, part of me was incredibly excited to get off this boat. I hated sailing. But the other part of me was horribly worried that we'd step into another trap or another situation where we were needing to run or fight for our lives. Still, I had to stay strong and courageous for my friends.

"See that small blue house over there?" Kilko said quietly.

I was sure she was keeping her voice down because who knew who could be lurking on the shore. Helena nodded and pointed the ship toward that area. I walked over to Kilko, who was leaning on the ship's railing. "Whose house is that? Where are we?" I asked quietly, trying to keep the noise down.

"The house belongs to an old friend of mine," Kilko said. "They don't live here anymore. In fact, no one does. They kept the house here in their name, in case of an emergency someday, and I would say this counts as an emergency. I know they'd be ok with me using their home."

"Where are we?" I asked, not recognizing this part of our kingdom.

"We're far north of the castle," Kilko answered. "If we head east, we'll end up at the Isle of Perdita, and if we head west, we'll end up in the top most part of the Zirkels. And south... well, south will take us to Crestwood."

Kilko was looking at the shore to see if we were going to be ambushed. I was hoping we wouldn't be, because the king would have had no way of contacting his allies on land to alert them about what had happened. He was hopefully still on that boat with the queen. Which meant they were far, far behind us.

I thought about that for a moment, about what might have happened to the king. Did Emmeria kill him? Or did he kill Emmeria? I didn't think they would have been able to peacefully co-exist on that boat. The fact was, we were fleeing from the two most powerful people in our world and we had exactly what they wanted right here: the Book of Viempro and Fern. It was a terrifying thought because the king and queen would have two armies to fight us, and we were only seven people. One of us was human, one was a Potens without his gift, and one was a small child. And then there were Kilko, Helena and Gregorio, who at least had gifts we could use, and me, with a gift that was of no use in a fight.

There were too many frightening things about our situation. The first was that literally everyone everywhere would be looking for us. Especially when news started to break that we were fugitives from the world's two most powerful people. No one would want to help us, because they would know that helping us would mean death. The second was that we really didn't have much of a plan, which meant that we would be just taking chances from one place to the next.

"We'll be safe here for a little while," Kilko said as Helena started to dock the boat. "It should give us just enough time to come up with a plan and recharge."

We needed a solid plan that would help us get ahead of the king and queen, and give us a chance to hide the Book of Viempro. We also needed to find more food and water. While the boat had food on it, it was running low, and if we were going to be on the run for a while, we'd need more supplies.

Both Gregorio and Bondi helped Kilko dock while Helena steered us in. Mikka, Fern and I looked over the side at the house: it had two stories, antique molding on the outside, and large windows with dark green curtains inside that you could see from out here. The house was painted a light blue, although the paint was peeling, and the dark green stood out against the pale color. The main door had a quaint-looking porch, the kind of porch I had always dreamed of having. It was covered and screened in, which meant you could sit outside for hours with no bugs and just enjoy the sounds of the forest.

My heart started to race. I felt anxious knowing that shore would mean unexpected company, if people found out where we were. At least on the boat we could see the danger coming and anticipate it. Shore would bring all new hazards.

"It's going to be ok," Mikka whispered.

I think he'd realized that I was starting to have a panic attack, because he put his hand in mine and squeezed tightly so I'd know he was there. I looked over at his ocean-blue eyes and managed to smirk at him to put on a confident front. He leaned over and kissed me on the forehead. Mikka was holding onto Fern with his other hand and I looked over at her, knowing that I had to be strong for her especially.

I took a deep breath, trying to calm my anxiety, but it was hard to move forward when it felt like every step we took was just another toward a new problem, rather than toward safety. The house looked lovely, but my brain couldn't stop from thinking about how we would have to leave here shortly anyway. It felt like we wouldn't be safe for too long. This boat was the only place I'd felt truly safe in a while, since we couldn't be attacked without seeing the threat first.

The boat had stopped moving. Gregorio and Bondi had tied ropes to a small wooden platform at the edge of the water so that the boat wouldn't drift away. Gregorio helped us all slowly get off of the boat one by one, and Kilko walked up to the house to grab a key from under the doormat. At least entering this house would be easy. No breaking in needed.

Kilko knocked four times but there was no answer. She put the key in, turned it and slightly opened the door. "Hello, it's me," she said, careful not to reveal her name. No one answered. She turned back to us, nodded, and we all headed into the home.

"Do you think we should move the boat?" Mikka said, looking back at it through the doorway before walking in. "It'll be obvious if someone sees it that this house is where we are."

"Normally I'd say yes," Kilko answered, "but it will be dark soon, so it will be hard to see. Plus, we won't be here for long."

That statement brought my anxiety right back. It was the never knowing where we would be next that made me anxious. I hated it. So I tried to distract myself by looking around inside of the house.

"Who's this friend of yours?" I said loudly, not on purpose. I was just in awe of how big the house was, even though it was out in the middle of actual nowhere.

"His name is Hilgo," Kilko said. "He's a bit paranoid. He built this house himself, every single thing in it he made by hand. He's a

Potens, his gift is in water movement, but his true gift, well, more like his talent, is carpentry."

The woodwork inside of the house was astonishing. The staircase was a winding one that went all the way to the top, with these beautiful carved wooden railings. There were hand-carved frames that had pictures of landscapes all throughout the house, not a single picture of a person or Potens. The carpets that lay on the floors contained intricate patterns which changed with each rug.

I was thankful that we would be here for a little while at least, although I knew I couldn't get too used to it. Kilko had us all move into the living room for safety, since it was better if we were all together in here rather than in the separate rooms throughout the house. While everyone got settled I walked into the kitchen, hoping that maybe, just maybe, there would be ingredients so that I could make us some tea.

A teapot sat on the counter. My heart jumped a little, I was so excited. I opened all the cabinets to see if I could find any herbs or spices, and to my luck there was a cabinet filled with them. There were more spices than I'd even had in my tea shop; I'd never seen this many varieties. I wanted to look through them all and see what was here, but I had to focus on the ones I needed for my recipe so I gathered up what I needed and placed them on the counter.

I started to boil the water and put together the different spices that would create the perfect healing tea. I grabbed seven mugs out of another cabinet and quickly rinsed them off (they had been collecting dirt over however long this place had been empty). I then pulled out cardamom, jasmine leaves and a bag of monkfruit, putting the perfect amount of spices into each cup. Once the water had boiled, I poured it into each mug, taking the time between pours to will the spices to work. The entire kitchen smelled like burning wood and cherry chocolate. I grabbed two mugs at a time and walked them into the living room where all my friends were, who immediately looked happy to smell the lovely scent of the healing tea.

"Here, it's a healing tea," I said as I passed the first two out to Kilko and Fern. "It should give you all your strength back." Kilko looked overjoyed.

"Here, let me help you," Mikka said, getting up to come with me and grab the rest. We walked into the kitchen, but when we were out of earshot of the rest of the group, Mikka pulled me close and gave me a kiss. I smiled, but then his expression changed. He hadn't just followed me in here to kiss me.

"I didn't want to say this in front of everyone else, but I'm really worried about what all this means for Fern," he said quietly as he hugged me for comfort.

I looked up at his beautiful blue eyes and said quietly, "I know. I think we need to find out more about what happens if she transfers the gift of immortality. Does it take life out of her, or does it just bring her back to what she was before she wandered into that forest? I bet Kilko knows where we can find more answers, so until then let's just keep Fern as safe as we can until we have more information."

Mikka nodded and kissed me on the forehead before grabbing more tea to bring back to the others. When we walked back in, they were already talking.

"I think we should take the castle from them and use it as a place of safety," Helena was saying. "It has strong walls."

"No," Bondi said. "They'll have to take it back, which will just put us in a bad spot. We'll have to fight and there's only seven of us. But if we keep running, we might not have to fight."

"But then what?" Gregorio asked. "We run forever? They're going to come after us eventually, they want the book. So how long are we going to keep this up? Plus, we don't even know if both of them survived back there, the king and Alco could be dead already."

"You do have a point," Bondi said with a puzzled expression. "We may end up on the run forever unless we can figure out a way to stop them for good." He looked at Helena for guidance.

"What else can the book do?" Helena asked.

Bondi and Gregorio looked at one another. "The book has several dark enchantments," Bondi explained. "Nothing in it should be read aloud by any of us."

"The whole thing is cursed in some way," Gregorio added. "Anyone who reads it aloud and uses it will forever be stained somehow with darkness."

So we couldn't use it against them then. We had to hide it, for good. Mikka and I passed out the tea so that everyone else would be able to drink it and feel its effects while we tried to figure out another way to stop the king and queen. We sat in silence as we drank, deep in thought.

I could see that everyone in the room was starting to feel and look better, so I decided to interrupt the silence. "Is there anything in the book about immortality?" I asked. I wanted to find a cure for Fern and find out how to keep her safe. While it was important to figure out our next step, if we could rid Fern of this then they wouldn't have a reason to need her.

"Unfortunately, no," Bondi said. "I looked through the entire thing and there is not one mention of it."

I let out a sigh.

"There is someone that might have more information on what we can do," Helena said. "I can't believe I didn't think of him sooner, but with the new information we got from Kilko, it made me realize that he might be a good source to ask. But he's all the way in Sutton, so it would be a long journey. We would have to either go back through the Zirkels or through Crestwood to get there, and I'm not sure that either of those paths would be worth it, especially if we get there and find out he doesn't know."

Helena got up to look out the window, and my heart sank for a moment because I thought she had seen something. But then she turned back around and sat back down with all of us.

"Who is this person and why do you think they would know?" Mikka chimed in.

"I've never met this person," explained Helena, "which is why I didn't think of them in the first place. But Dova would talk of him frequently, his name is Julian. He knew Dova and supported what she was doing in the Zirkels, hiding powerful Potens. He would send us baskets of food on carts that he pushed through the woods with his gift. Dova once said that he was obsessed with history and ancient stories, so I thought he might be our best bet on finding out more when Kilko brought up that story she had heard."

It seemed like a good plan, but the last time we were in that area Lintown had been destroyed. It was only a matter of time until that happened to Sutton. It might have already happened.

"I don't think Sutton exists anymore," Mikka said, looking at me. "Evergreen and I were near there when we left Kinver, and a few hours later Lintown was completely gone. I can't imagine Sutton still stands, that was long ago now."

I thought back on our journey from Kinver to Crestwood when I'd first met Mikka. It felt like such a long time ago now.

Helena looked frustrated for a moment, but then her expression changed. "Well that is good news," she said.

I was confused. How could it be good news that the town might have been destroyed?

"If the town is empty, then I'm sure that Julian will be there alone," Helena explained with a smile. "Dova always used to tell us that he's not the running type, he's more the hiding type. He was supposed to join us in the Zirkels but then everything happened, so I would bet he's still in Sutton, using all the resources he can from the town. Sutton has a massive library, and that's where Dova said he always spent his time. Now that it's empty, he's probably just enjoying having it all to himself."

"But, and I hate to ask this, what if he's dead?" Bondi said. He wasn't wrong.

"If he's dead, then we have an entire empty town to ourselves," Kilko pointed out. "It's a place that they wouldn't think to look for us too, because it's away from the castle and back toward Kinver."

"We can also look in the library if he's not there for any old stories that match the one Kilko heard," Helena added.

I nodded. Everyone was in agreement. Sutton was the plan ahead.

We sat around in the living room for a while, trying to come up with a plan for how to safely get to Sutton. It was harder than we'd thought. It wasn't going well because nearly every plan someone suggested put us in some sort of danger. It was just a matter of which suggestion put us in the least amount of danger. Trying to decide between immediate death and potential death was a frustrating thought, and there were just no options that were completely safe.

"What choice do we have?" Mikka finally said to the group.

Everyone looked around at each other and then back to Mikka. They all had worried expressions on their faces because there was not one suggestion that didn't have death as a possible outcome. But we all knew that staying here would be worse and that there was really no other choice but to leave. All of the options were dangerous, but staying here and being found by the queen or the king would have been worse than all those options combined. Because staying, well, that meant death for sure. We would just have to rely on the hope that we would make it, one step at a time.

The dread of this decision held heavy in the air, but we knew deep down that leaving would be the safest choice (which was really saying something). I thought for a moment about if there even was a slightly safe option to choose, but we had really exhausted all ideas.

"I think the Zirkels are our best option back," Helena said firmly.

Bondi looked frustrated when his brother nodded in agreement with Helena. "Do you remember what it was like, living there?" Bondi asked with a tone in his voice as if he was shocked that she would even suggest it.

Gregorio looked off into the distance, thinking deeply about that statement, but Helena interrupted Gregorio's thoughts. The second she spoke, Gregorio looked like he was fully back here and present.

"Yeah, I do, but I also remember what our journey at Crestwood, at the king's castle, was like too," Helena said. "And I can tell you with certainty that there is no way that the castle isn't going to be on high alert, especially if they see us coming. And yes, the Zirkels were awful, but at least they're familiar."

Gregorio looked at Helena and shrugged. "You always were good at scouting the forest, Helena," he said with a smile. Helena didn't smile back, but she nodded.

"Are you two forgetting that we relied heavily on my gift, to shock any creatures that came our way?" Bondi asked. "We don't have that option now."

I realized in that moment that it wasn't going back to the Zirkels that had Bondi worried, but going back when he had no gift anymore to help.

"What if we just went through the Forest of Embers, on the very outside of Crestwood, and used that to travel to Halvar? That would bring us back to the towns where we could head south to Sutton?" Mikka's voice trailed off in uncertainty. It would be a long journey either way, but it was an alternative.

"I think we should go on the Chero Trail," I said, considering all of our options. "You know, the popular backpacking trail that's just on the outside of the Zirkels? That at least would keep us away from the castle, out of the towns, and out of the Zirkels. If we needed to hide, we could hop right into the Zirkels which, although dangerous, would mean no one would probably follow. Plus, are there really that many Crawlers that live on the very edge of the forest?"

Helena looked at me with a surprised expression, like she hadn't thought of that idea. I knew it wasn't a great option——the trail was long and right next to danger at all times——but it was an actual trail. The idea that we would be able to hop into the Zirkels if needed made me feel a little safer too, knowing that we would be able to escape from whoever we'd need to. Even though the Zirkels was never a safe option, it felt like knowing what we would have to face was better than not knowing.

"Not a bad idea, Evergreen," Kilko said. Helena, Gregorio, Bondi and Mikka nodded.

Fern was sitting in silence, drinking her tea. I didn't actually think she was even listening to us; she was so focused on her tea cup that it was almost surprising to see how calm she was able to make herself. I cringed a little, knowing that it was probably because of all that she had endured, that this was the way she'd found to deal with it. I thought of what Kilko had said, that Fern possessed gifts we hadn't seen yet, and that idea made me feel both safe and unsettled. I didn't know what kind of power Fern possessed, but we had to hope that it would reveal itself if we ever needed it.

"Well, that's settled then," Kilko said. "We leave at dawn."

She walked off to head up the beautiful staircase, and the noise picked up as the group started to have conversations about how to protect ourselves, methods of fighting, different things we all had learned. Helena was sharing information on war tactics and how to effectively attack a small group. Gregorio and Bondi were talking about using the element of surprise.

I found a moment to pull Mikka aside. "Mikka, can I talk to you for a minute?" I whispered. He nodded. We both got up and headed into the kitchen again to talk. Once we were out of earshot of the rest of our friends, I grabbed his hand gently. "What do you want to do with Fern?" I asked.

He looked at me. "What do you mean?" he whispered back, almost looking frightened of what I might say next.

"Well, they don't have the book or Fern, so no one can use her to make themselves immortal" I said. "But I was thinking we should come up with a plan for what to do if we all somehow get caught, to get Fern safely away in a moment's notice if needed." I knew this would be hard for him to hear, but we had to think everything through.

Mikka's face changed from frightened to confused. "Well, if something happens, I could always take her into the Zirkels on my own," he said with uncertainty.

I was sure he knew that him bringing her into the forest would be the most obvious option, and one that would most certainly not be safe. He was only human after all, and that could only get him so far when fighting a powerful Potens. I leaned in to ensure no one would overhear my whisper.

"I think you should ask Helena to take Fern if anything goes wrong. She has the strongest gift here and could ensure Fern's safety."

Helena's gift could kill anyone in an instant. She had also somehow been able to free herself from that Potens circle on the boat. She had more power than anyone, and would be able to keep Fern safe.

Mikka looked confused. "I can't leave her," he said.

I nodded. "I know it would be hard, but I think you should ask Helena and not let anyone else know. This way, if we ever find ourselves in trouble, no one can be forced to tell where they went." I spoke softly, trying to get him to understand that it would be for the best if he let this be the backup plan. If we were captured and the book was taken, this would buy us time. Mikka finally nodded and kissed me on the forehead. He knew that this was a good idea, and the best option to keep Fern safe.

We grabbed some freeze-dried snacks from the cabinets and headed back into the living room. Everyone was done with their tea by now and they all seemed well rested and re-energized. Kilko came down the stairs with two backpacks, both completely stuffed. One was a deep blue color and the other was forest green.

"Whatcha got in those?" Bondi said with a mouth full of the snacks that we'd just brought in. Gregorio let out a low chuckle at his brother, and we all laughed. It was the first time in a long time that we'd all heard laughter fill the room and, for just a moment, we were able to forget about the situation we were in.

Kilko smiled briefly before going back to her stern expression. She seemed like the kind of person that wasn't interested in letting her guard down for even a moment, and she wanted us to listen to what she would say. She waited for everyone to stop laughing before she spoke.

"I knew that there would be survival supplies upstairs, so I packed two bags full of them." She lifted up the one in her right hand, which was deep blue. "This one has a small hatchet, an emergency blanket, packs of freeze-dried food, two aluminum cups and loose-leaf tea." She paused for a moment to glance over at me. I nodded, thankful that she had thought about that for me. "And it also has a few bottles of water," she added, before lifting the forest green bag in her left hand. "This one has a small first aid kit, a few different potions which are labeled——please read the label before you use them for anything——and a rolled up sack of twelve knives. The potions take up most of the space in this bag, but I think they could be useful. I have no idea who made them, but we'll have to trust that my friend who lived here didn't label them wrong." She shrugged.

Gregorio let out another laugh, but Kilko's facial expression showed that she wasn't joking so he quickly went back to being silent.

"I'll need one of you to carry one of the bags," Kilko said. "I'll take the other. I'll put the book in mine."

"I've got it," Mikka volunteered.

"Perfect," Kilko said. "Get some rest. I'll take first watch and then we leave at dawn."

We had decided that we would all sleep in this room together, having someone take watch every hour like we'd done on the ship. Separation would be dangerous so we had to stick together for now. Kilko handed out blankets and pillows to us all, and I laid my head down to get some rest.

I awoke to a gentle shake from Mikka.

"Time to go," he said softly, while the others all rummaged around to gather a few additional supplies before we left. I sat up, letting out a big yawn.

"Sleepyhead," Mikka said as he helped me to my feet.

I remembered those days when we sat in the forest, only running from the king. Not toward anything, not because we were trying to save our kingdom, but just because we were both in trouble. Those moments had felt terrifying then, but now I realized they were much better than where we were now. I realized I hadn't even had a panic attack in a while, that we hadn't had enough time to relax for me to even feel the panic coming on. It was a weird feeling, to know that the anxiety would always be there but that it hadn't been that bad lately, even though I'd been in more danger now than ever before. Survival mode had kicked in and my anxiety had taken a back seat.

I let the thought drift away as I helped pack a few things away into the backpacks. I grabbed two knives and put a small snack in one bag. I also looked through the tea Kilko had packed and realized she knew more about tea brewing then I'd thought. She had everything we needed to make healing tea, a forgetful-draught and a sleeping-draught. I was impressed.

We all headed out of the door that faced the ocean. I still couldn't see any other ships, so hopefully we were in the clear. The sun was just peeking over the horizon – it was time to go, before anyone could spot the ship from the water. We took one last look at the ocean, the waves, the horizon, and headed back behind the house into the forest.

The forest was much more dense than the one by Kinver. Maybe more trees were able to grow because it was so close to the water? I couldn't be sure.

We walked in two lines, trying to keep watch for each other as we traveled. I was in one line with Bondi leading, me right behind him, Fern behind me and Helena last. The other line was led by Gregorio, followed by Kilko and then Mikka.

I kept looking over toward him, wondering if he had asked Helena what I'd told him to ask her, but I wasn't sure because he kept looking around frantically. He also hadn't said anything to me if he had, which was all for the better because the fewer people that knew, the safer Fern would be if they had to escape.

We kept quiet as we walked. Although this wasn't the Zirkels, we hadn't been in these woods yet and who knew what had happened since we'd last been in this area. I looked at the ground to make sure I wouldn't trip over any branches, while glancing up at our surroundings every once in a while to check for anyone who might be following us. Or any*thing*.

My heart was racing. Not now, please not now. But there would always be time for a panic attack. My anxiety started to fill my chest, like an unbelievable weight was laying on me. It was getting harder to breathe. So much for this not being so bad lately. There wasn't even anything that was causing this panic attack, I think it was just being under this type of pressure for so long.

I stopped walking and crouched down for a moment. Mikka walked over, gesturing for everyone else to keep going. He put his hand on my chest to show me it would be ok, holding it over my heart while he instructed me to breathe slowly. We sat and counted breaths: one, two, three, four, five on an inhale and one, two, three, four, five on an exhale. I felt my heartbeat slow back down after a few moments, felt the ground beneath me become sturdy and steady. I could take deep breaths again without feeling like I was drowning.

"You're going to be ok, Ever," Mikka said slowly as he helped me back up to my feet.

I felt embarrassed to have had a panic attack but I didn't have time to feel that now, we had to catch back up to our group. "Thank you," I whispered as I wiped the leaves off of my pants and grabbed his hand so we could rush to catch up to them. It had only been a few minutes so they couldn't have gotten too far, but we couldn't see them.

"Where are they?" Mikka whispered, worried since Fern was with them. We started to run but they weren't there. "FERN!" Mikka shouted through a whisper, trying to be quiet but also trying to get an answer.

A pinecone hit my head, hard. I looked up and all of our friends were in branches of different trees. "What the... " I said, grabbing Mikka's shirt so that he would look up. Helena was frantically waving for us to get in a tree. Without another word, we climbed. I was almost at the top when a branch broke under my foot and fell to the ground with a loud thud.

"Did you hear that?" said a voice not too far away.

"I know they're here somewhere," another voice said. "I heard one of them shout a moment ago."

"You can't hide," said a third voice in a sing-song tone.

"We heard you," said a fourth voice, this one even closer.

Helena was holding Fern tightly and covering her mouth as if to prevent her from crying or making a sound. I stayed as still as possible, but a bead of sweat was trickling down my face. I reached up to wipe it off and then peered through the coverage of the leaves to see if I could see any of the people below.

Four King's Guard, all dressed in golden armor, loudly moved below with no regard for their steps. They weren't worried about being discovered, in fact it was like they wanted everyone to know they were there. They had their bows and arrows ready in each of their hands, and were all carrying an extra quiver of arrows.

Looking at their golden suits was blinding enough, but then the sun caught the reflection of one item so brightly that it made me close my eyes for a moment. One of them had a dagger made of pure gold strapped to his side.

*My dagger.*

They must have caught up with Jay, the man that had made the blood oath with Dova when we borrowed his boat so long ago. For a moment I wondered what had happened to him. He must have been killed, or sided with them. Either way, that was my dagger on that Kingsman. I wanted it back. I grabbed Mikka's hand lightly, to get his attention and to point at the dagger. He mouthed the word

"NO" at me. I knew we couldn't reveal ourselves just for the dagger, but if we had to fight them, I would try to get it.

The guards walked closer until they were right underneath us. They stopped moving. Another bead of sweat started to trickle down my face, but I was too afraid to move to wipe it off. It slowly fell off of my face and dropped down, down, down.

The bead of sweat hit one of their helmets, causing them to look right up at us.

It all happened so fast. The fear bubbled up inside all of us as the Kingsmen pointed their arrows right up in our direction. But, just a moment later, they were all lying flat on the ground, sleeping. I looked over at Kilko, who had her arms out. I realized that she had used her gift to put them to sleep. She smiled back at me and said, "Hurry."

We all rushed down out of the trees. I walked over to the guard carrying the golden dagger that my grandfather had made for me, grabbed it and placed it in my belt loop. It was mine again. Without my golden axe, the dagger made me feel whole once more. It was my family's, and with it I felt a connection to them that I couldn't describe. After all, it was all I had left of them.

We all started to run through the forest as quickly as we could. We only had a few more miles until we reached the Chero Trail, a place with more cover and a sense of familiarity for some of us. There, at least, we might feel some sort of safety.

"How did they find us?" I said, out of breath as we ran.

"I'm not sure," Helena said as she continued to run, "but I don't want to stay here long enough to find out that there could be more of them."

Gregorio put Fern on his back, to allow us to move faster. Those guards worked for the king, the golden armor gave it away. But how would the Kingsmen know we were back in this kingdom if the king had died in Melted Cor by the Queen? The thought made me nervous because it meant some of the king's group did survive. A chill ran down my spine. We should have killed him when we had the chance.

"We have to keep moving, quicker!" Kilko shouted.

We all ran as fast as we could to keep a steady, quick pace. I was exhausted, but I knew everyone else probably was too, and none of them were giving up so I couldn't either.

After an hour of running, or so it felt like, we reached the edge of the Chero Trail. We'd arrived at the northernmost entrance, where there was a small, carved wooden sign signifying the start of the trail itself. It read: CHERO TRAIL, 100 MILES NORTH TO SOUTH. One hundred miles felt like a lot, especially after that run.

We all darted into the trailhead. I didn't really understand why this was a popular trail, because there were so many stories of people disappearing here. One side was thick trees, all leading to different towns depending on where you were, and the other side was pure darkness leading into the Zirkels, where hikers would often get swept away. Unfortunately for us, we'd have to make camp slightly inside the territory of the Zirkels, to protect us from being seen by anyone on the outside. While in our situation that was better than the alternative of staying somewhere and being killed, I couldn't quite wrap my head around the idea that humans would stay here for fun. And although being this close to the Zirkels would protect us from most humans, it would not protect us from what lay in the forest.

Crawlers.

The idea sent a shiver down my spine. I remembered the feeling I'd had the first time I saw them in person. Realistically, they weren't the scariest thing I'd seen since then, but the way they moved and their size made my stomach curl. I sent that thought quickly away and continued to move with the group.

The sun was almost low enough that it would be sunset soon. This day had gone by as if it were no time at all, but we had made a lot of progress on our journey today. More than we would have if we hadn't been sprinting for our lives. We had been moving swiftly for hours now, and we still had to make it a bit farther into the trail in order to find a safe place to camp. Especially after those King's Guard had showed up.

The trail was desolate. Typically during this time of year—fall—the trail was filled with excited backpackers on their overnight journeys. There were always people who talked about this trail being the be-all and end-all for backpackers, a true test of will and skill to hike the whole thing. I still thought it was a silly place for people to be backpacking with this kind of danger on one side of it. But maybe that was the thrill of it all. We'd be doing it, but not for fun, and having to run through this trail with few supplies, little food, and with it actually being a life or death situation made it really impossible to enjoy at all.

"We'll take this another three miles or so, and then we can stop for a short rest," Kilko said. "I'm thinking we rest for two hours at a time; that will at least keep distance between us and whoever is after us."

We all nodded in unison. It would be hard to sleep for just a few hours and feel rested, but we didn't have a choice. To rest for too long meant giving other people more time to catch up with us, and that was something we couldn't risk.

Just three more miles and I could rest my feet. I moved quickly, trying to keep up with the group, and as I did I reached down to feel my dagger. It felt good to have it back, although at what cost? We were almost found and killed before Kilko saved us. At least Kilko could put people to sleep rather than kill them. I liked that idea, it made me feel like we weren't turning into the same people as the king or queen.

I ran to catch up to her and whispered, "Kilko, can I talk to you privately?" She nodded and we ran slightly ahead of the group, so the movement forward and our slight distance would prevent anyone from hearing. "What do you know about Fern transferring her immortality?" I said, looking back to make sure we were out of earshot.

"Not much, to be honest," she said, "but what I do know is that it's probably only been done less than a handful of times. No matter what we find out about it, the results might not be the same for her or whoever she transfers it to." She moved in a little closer. "The other thing is that it takes a great amount of energy to transfer something like that. It could probably be done only once, meaning it couldn't be undone. The thing that worries me is that we don't know what the effects would be for Fern if she did it."

I nodded, understanding what she meant. Without saying it outright, she wanted me to know that Fern might not survive if she were to transfer her immortality. But there had to be some way for us to do it safely so that Fern wouldn't be in danger. And that meant we could never let either the king or the queen do it.

We slowed our pace to allow the group to catch up with us. I was exhausted now. We'd been running for miles and miles and we still had a lot further to go before we reached Sutton. But at least we'd rest shortly.

After about another hour had gone by, Kilko slowed to a stop.

"Alright, let's rest for a bit," she said, looking around to make sure we weren't being followed.

Not a person or Potens in sight. The sounds of the forest were the only thing we could hear, and I felt comforted by the normal noise of animals and birds from the trees that lined the outskirts of the town. But on the other side of the trail, the Zirkels, there was pure silence, that kind of silence that became deafening if you got too close. I moved a bit further away from that side.

Mikka had started to remove his pack when Kilko stopped him. "Not here," she said. "We can't rest here." Mikka looked confused, because she'd just said to stop, but Kilko had turned to face the dark forest to our right. The fog that wove through the forest was still just as terrifying as the first time I'd seen the Zirkels, back with Mikka when we escaped from Lintown.

"In here," Kilko said, reaching into the side of her pack to grab out a large knife. She stepped directly into the fog, making us unable to see her.

I didn't want to camp in the darkness, I'd only meant for us to go in there if we were avoiding someone. This definitely was not what I'd meant by suggesting we use this trail.

"Kilko," I said softly, to not attract attention from anyone in the other side of the woods.

"I'm fine, come in," she said.

We all looked at one another. We had known deep down that this was the safer plan, but choosing to go back into the Zirkels was not an easy choice to make. Helena, Gregorio and Bondi didn't look quite as scared, maybe because they had lived here for a while with Dova. I nodded at the group, signaling that I would be going in. I took a step into the fog, heart racing but with no better options than this one.

I closed my eyes as I took that first step, but when I opened them I couldn't see Kilko. Instead, I saw a pair of luminescent yellow eyes peering at me through the darkness.

# 17

The eyes startled me. Where on earth was Kilko, and what was this creature that was watching me? I knew it wasn't a Crawler because the eyes were different, but it didn't really matter what it was because I didn't have any great powers. I tried to shout for help through the fog but Kilko and the others didn't answer. I couldn't see them and I couldn't turn around.

"Help!" I shouted again, but there was no answer. "Mikka!" I pleaded, but was met with nothing but silence.

A wisp of wind came out of nowhere. It had to be Gregorio, but the wind was doing nothing to the creature. It stepped closer and closer, until I could make out what it was: a wolf stood in front of me. Not an unusual animal for the forest, but it was massive. I couldn't figure out if that was because I was so scared or because the wolf was actually huge. Its eyes glowed so brightly it was hard to look straight at it. I grabbed my dagger and gripped it tightly, ready to defend myself if needed.

Then, from behind me, I felt a hand grab my free one. Mikka.

"Helena, hold Fern and stay out of here for a moment," he said gently.

The wolf lunged forward with its mouth open, ready to devour us. I held my dagger up toward it, ready to strike, just as Mikka pushed me out of the way. But the moment before the wolf chomped down on us, it abruptly fell to the ground, asleep. Kilko jumped down from a tree.

"Why didn't you answer me?" I said, pleading, as I tried to steady my breath. We'd almost just been eaten.

"I climbed the tree to look for a place to camp when you came in," Kilko said, also out of breath. "I heard you yell out so I came back as fast as I could."

"I didn't hear you clearly, it was weird you almost sounded muffled," Mikka said. The Zirkels were a weird place.

Mikka gestured through the fog to let the others know to come through. Helena looked at us with uncertainty as she appeared. I realized why Helena hadn't followed us in, Mikka must have asked her to keep Fern safe above all else.

"You made a lot of noise," she said. "I'm not sure we should stay here."

The words echoed through my head. I needed to rest so badly but she was right. We had made too much noise, and where there's one wolf, there are usually more.

"We have to keep going," Helena continued. We all nodded.

We decided to stay in the Zirkels but walk at the very edge, to prevent ourselves being seen from the outside but to also have a swift exit if we needed one. We ran as quick as we could along the tree line, exhaustion covering us all. But we were out of options to slow down now and we all knew we would be able to rest soon, which made hurrying up much more enticing.

"How much longer?" Fern said quietly from the middle of our group.

"Not too much longer, little one," Mikka said as he squeezed her hand a bit tighter.

I knew how he felt. I was certain that he was worried about what would happen to her and was holding on tightly to show that he didn't want to let go. I wouldn't let him lose her, to anything. I had lost my entire family and I wouldn't let it happen to Mikka, too. So although I was tired I had to push through, to be a good example for Fern.

We had been moving for another hour when Helena interrupted the silence.

"Here," she said.

She pointed to a dense area with quite a bit of tree and bush cover on all sides, and we followed her to the spot she had in mind for our camp. We were deeper into the Chero Trail than we had planned to be, so we were making good time. it didn't matter though because it was still quite a long journey ahead tomorrow.

Small rocks and twigs stuck out from the cold, damp floor, so we all laid out leaves to make the floor more comfortable to rest on. Unfortunately for us we didn't have any tents or sleeping bags, but we did have two small blankets. They were thin but they were better than nothing. We gave them both to Fern so she could rest comfortably.

Mikka started working to get a fire going but it was difficult with the moist air of the Zirkels. Bondi had decided that he would take first watch, but was gathering kindling before taking his post. Helena and Fern were sitting down together on a log and Helena was telling Fern about different defensive moves, to help prepare her for what might come. Kilko was patrolling around us into the

Chero Trail, setting up a perimeter to make sure we were safe. Gregorio was doing the same, but further into the Zirkels.

I took out a small pot so that I could prepare some healing tea once Mikka was able to get the fire going. I pulled out the tea ingredients and some food rations to hand out as well. I began dividing the dried fruit and jerky we had found at the house to give everyone a small portion. We would have to keep our energy up to be able to fight whoever might come our way. I would have killed for some fresh food right now, like a cooked deer or even a rabbit, but we didn't have the time to hunt because if someone found us, it would all go to waste.

Mikka finally got the fire going and I walked over with the pot. I brought the tea leaves and the special spices and herbs that Kilko had taken from the house. They were already ground down into a powder, which made them more potent.

"You ok?" I said to Mikka, who had a stoic expression on his face as he stoked the fire with a stick.

While the fire wouldn't be seen from the Chero Trail, it might attract things in the forest. But we were willing to take that chance for a bit, to at least get the tea going and build our strength back. Plus, it was nice to feel the warmth of the flames in this dark, cold place.

"Yeah, I'm fine," he said, continuing to poke the fire to help get it going. "I'm just thinking."

"What are you thinking about?" I asked.

He scrunched his face in thought. "I feel like we're missing something," he said.

"What do you mean?"

By this point, Helena had overhead and brought Fern over to get closer to us. They stood next to us as we continued to talk.

"Well, how would someone know that Fern was immortal in the

first place? I mean, I didn't even know... " Mikka said, his voice trailing off.

It was a good point. "I don't know, maybe the Tree Witch told someone?" I said.

A small voice interrupted. "I didn't even know," Fern said, holding Helena's hand.

"Yeah, but it does bring up the question of why the Tree Witch would tell someone," Helena said. "They usually don't like to reveal their secrets. Plus, it wouldn't do anyone any good to know that they were able to make people or Potens immortal."

"I'm not sure, but maybe when we get to Sutton we'll get the answer to more of these questions," Mikka said.

Kilko walked in from the woods, having overheard the end of our conversation.

"Like I said, I knew that Fern was the one from that story when I met her and put all of it together," Kilko explained. "I think if the king had heard that tale, maybe he figured it out too somehow. He does have a lot of spies in the kingdom, so it's possible someone told him about what happened to Fern when she was little."

I looked at Mikka as he continued to poke the fire, his gaze on Fern. It was confusing, the immortality, the book, all of it.

"Yeah, maybe," Mikka finally said. "I just feel like someone, somewhere, told him."

Kilko shrugged. It didn't really matter how the king had found out, because he knew and we couldn't undo that.

I poured water into the pot and set it to boil before willing the water and the tea leaves together. They released the wonderful smell of burning wood and cherry chocolate, making me feel instant relief. I hoped this tea would help us all feel recovered after such a long day of running to get here. We still had such a long way to go and didn't have time to be tired.

Bondi had moved a few larger logs around the fire as seats, where both Helena and Fern were now sitting to be closer to the warmth. Gregorio walked in through the bushes and also sat down on one of the logs.

"All clear for a few miles in," he said, looking over at Kilko to check on the Chero Trail.

"It was all good out there as well," she said. "We should be able to rest here for a few hours and regain our strength." She sat down on a log now too.

Mikka continued to stoke the fire as I waited for the tea to finish. Once the pot had cooled enough, I passed it around for everyone to have a sip. You could feel the relief in the air, everyone feeling better with food and tea in their bellies. We sat around the fire for a bit, not talking, just enjoying the warmth of the flames.

The crackle of the fire was the only thing making any noise over in this part of the forest. The Zirkels, after all, were a frightening place to be. Every once in a while, the sound of a wolf's howl would echo in the distance, and we could hear the sounds of other things—I wasn't even sure what they were—crying in the distance. But then it would go back to that crazy silence. At least the crackle of the fire was soothing, it always had been. It reminded me of camping.

Mikka, Fern, Helena, Kilko and Gregorio decided to sleep, but I chose to stay up by the fire with Bondi. I figured it would help if two people were awake and could keep each other up.

"How are you doing?" I whispered to him.

His facial expression showed that he knew the deeper meaning to the question I was asking. I wanted to know how he was doing after all this time without his gift. He had lost it, and life without it must have been a difficult adjustment. Especially considering he'd had such a powerful gift, to summon lightning.

"I'm fine," he said quietly, to avoid waking the rest of the group. "I just want this all to be over with so I can figure out my life." I nodded and he went on. "I just feel like this whole thing has been us running and losing. Like sure, we have Fern and the book, but how are we going to hide the book? How are we going to protect Fern? We have three Potens in our group that can protect us, and me... I'm practically useless."

It stung. I knew he didn't mean to hurt my feelings but I had always struggled with the fact that I didn't have a great gift. I loved my power, but to others it must have looked like just that too, useless.

Bondi saw my facial expression change. "Hey, Evergreen, I'm sorry," he said. "I didn't mean it like that. I just, I'm just getting used to my new life, that's all."

I nodded, thinking about what it must have been like for him. I had always felt this way so I was used to it. But I also knew now that while a gift might be great, courage mattered more. Because we all had made it this far, together.

We both stared into the fire and waited for our turn to rest.

# 18

I woke up and everyone was gone. It was just me in the Sunken Forest, which made no sense. We weren't even close to there.

"Mikka?" I said loudly.

I could hear the wind picking up, almost drowning out my cries. I started to panic. I ran, but it was almost like I was going nowhere. I just ran in the same spot, over and over again until I started to tire. I looked around frantically, trying to see where my friends had gone, but they were nowhere to be found.

"MIKKA!" I cried loudly.

I turned around to see a figure. It was enveloping our surroundings in darkness.

"MIKKA!" I shouted.

The darkness came closer, and closer.

I screamed.

"Evergreen! Wake up, you're ok," Mikka said as he gently woke me.

I had been dreaming. Dreaming. A path-dream.

"What was that?" Mikka asked.

"It felt like a type of a dream that I've had before," I explained as I reached for my golden dagger. "Dova said that the gold in my dagger is infused with sight. I just got the dagger back, so I must have had a path-dream."

My heart was racing. I couldn't quite figure out what the dream had meant. I spent the next few minutes explaining it to Mikka and everyone else, but none of us could figure out what to make of it. We knew though that we had to pay close attention if I had another one.

When I finally stood up, Mikka hugged me, knowing I had been scared. It was still dark out and everything around me looked the same, but the fire was dying out. Everyone was packing up our stuff to get moving. As we got ready to go, Mikka explained path-dreams to Kilko.

"I've never heard of path-dreams," she said.

Helena looked surprised since she thought Kilko knew everything.

"Yeah, we hadn't either until Dova told us about them when Evergreen was first having them because of her axe," Mikka said. "The problem is, the last time she had them someone died. We have to pay close attention if she has one again." Kilko nodded.

I was frustrated. To have another path-dream meant that something like the dream was coming. It felt terrifying because the darkness in my dream had made my skin crawl. I wasn't looking forward to having that dream again but I knew I'd have to if we were going to figure out what it meant. We would need to get more information from it.

Mikka put one of the packs back on, and this time Gregorio took the other from Kilko. Helena put out the fire with just a small bit of water – the last thing we needed was a forest fire right now on top of everything else we were dealing with. Luckily the air here was damp, so the fire went out quickly.

"Alright, let's move," Kilko said. We headed back onto the Chero trail.

We all nodded in agreement as Kilko and Helena moved to the front. Gregorio and Bondi took places at the back while Fern, Mikka and I were in the center of the group. We would all look out for any trouble that might come our way from all directions, trying to be as prepared as possible.

At this rate, it would still be days until we made it to Sutton. It was impossible to go much faster than walking at this point because we couldn't keep running for days straight without exhausting ourselves. We also couldn't risk using all of our energy running because if we needed to fight someone––or something––along the way, we would need our strength. I couldn't just keep brewing healing teas every few hours since it took time to start a fire and will the tea together. We also wanted to save those ingredients for when we really needed them.

The path ahead of us was filled with leaves. Literally, leaves all over. Fall was my favorite season but the crunchy leaves on the ground were making it impossible to walk without making a ton of noise. I realized that if someone was trying to get us, it would be obvious with all the noise we were making walking on the trail. But the Chero Trail was better than being even a foot further into the Zirkels than we had to be. One night in there was enough.

Suddenly, there was a loud snap from behind us. We all immediately stopped moving, to see if it was one of us that had stepped on a branch.

"What... was... that?" I whispered to Mikka.

As we swiveled our heads around to prevent ourselves from moving and making any more noise, I reached for the dagger on my belt loop. I held it up in my hand, ready for what might come.

Kilko, Helena and Gregorio all had their arms up and were readying themselves to use their gifts. Gregorio transformed into wind and disappeared, probably trying to see which direction the noise had come from and assess if it was a threat. Moments of stillness passed as we all stood, frozen in time, waiting to see where he'd gone.

He appeared out of nowhere.

"RUN!" he shouted through lost breath. He was panting like he had been running, even though he had been wind for just a moment.

Danger. We were in danger.

Clouds started to appear above, quickly getting dark and dense. We started sprinting as small rain drops began to hit our heads. The rain got heavier and heavier until we were all sprinting through mud, caught in a massive rainstorm. Thunder roared from above, releasing a crack that felt like it shook the earth. Lightning struck the trees around us and I realized that the rainstorm must have been from a Potens that was after us. We had to keep running.

Helena and Kilko ran to the back of our group to defend us from what was coming: four horses, each carrying a King's Guard in golden armor. Their flags of the king were held high, the soldiers were stampeding towards us through the rain. One of them had their arms outstretched, causing the storm that was limiting our vision.

Kilko threw out her hands to put them to sleep, but out of nowhere she was holding her throat, like she was choking. Helena tried next, her eyes glowing red as they got closer and closer, but then she was suddenly flung into a tree. Gregorio tried to transform into a wind again but the storm around us was so strong that he was stuck in the one place.

These were horrifying gifts that the knights were displaying. They must all be Potens, working under the king's orders. And all of our best-gifted Potens were out of options. I could only hold my dagger high, ready to fight the knights as they got closer to us.

Fern was left standing right in the middle of the trail, soaking wet and shivering. The horses were running straight towards her. Mikka stepped in front to shield her but he was knocked off of his feet by a gift from one of the Potens on horseback. He screamed for his sister as he tried to get back to his feet. The sound of thunder got louder and fiercer. It was hard to keep my eyes open, the rain was heavy. But I saw as Fern closed her eyes, tightened her fists and screamed at the top of her lungs.

Her scream was louder than the thunder.

If I hadn't been standing three feet from it all, watching it all happen, I wouldn't have believed it. The four knights on horseback were gone. Vanished. But their horses were still there, looking confused at where their riders had gone. The storm around us stopped abruptly and the sun came back out to warm us.

Helena and Kilko had managed to get up and rush over. "What happened?" they said in unison, also not believing what they'd seen.

"Fern screamed and they were gone," I said, in total disbelief of the words coming out of my mouth. I couldn't believe that this little girl had somehow just vanished those Potens with some kind of great power. "Fern, what did you do?" I said calmly, so that she wouldn't feel overwhelmed. I didn't want her to think she was in any trouble, I just wanted to see if she knew how she'd done that.

Fern stood there with tears in her eyes. "I... I don't know. I just pictured them somewhere else," she said.

"Where?" Mikka asked. He looked concerned.

"I pictured them in the water," Fern said. Bondi and Gregorio looked at each other.

Everyone seemed confused. That wasn't a gift, that was something else. We now knew for sure that Fern had secrets that we didn't know about. But I couldn't believe that she'd literally just vanished those people to somewhere else. I thought about what her experience with the Tree Witch must have been like all those years ago, when she was so much smaller. Not many had run into a Tree Witch and live, so I couldn't think of what the witch might have done to her.

Mikka looked like he wanted to throw up. His only family left was not just immortal but something else. Even Helena looked slightly terrified of Fern, but also in awe. She had saved us.

"Well, we should all be thanking Fern," Helena said as she started brushing herself off after hitting the ground and the tree. "Without her, we'd all be dead."

No one spoke for a little while as we all processed what had happened. Finally, Bondi and Gregorio rallied up the horses. If the Kingsmen were gone, we might as well take their horses because it would shorten our trip to Sutton. Four horses, seven of us, so we'd be able to have three horses carrying two people each and one person riding on their own. It would be much better than walking.

Before we could mount though, Kilko pulled me and Mikka off to the side. "What was that?" she asked with fear in her voice.

Mikka shook his head. "I have no idea," he said, before adding, "But she's not a Potens."

Kilko touched her hand to her head in disbelief. "Ok, well, I don't know what happened but I do hope that wherever she vanished those Kingsmen to they can't escape, because if anyone finds out about this we'll have more than just the king and queen to worry about."

She was right, this was beyond the realm of gifts that any of us had seen. I mean sure, there are Potens with powerful abilities that can kill, but this... this was something way beyond that. This was old magic, the kind that hadn't existed in centuries. Whatever happened with Fern and that Tree Witch, it must have given her something different.

"More of a reason to hurry to Sutton," I said, realizing that we now had more questions than answers. I was thankful for what

Fern had done but I felt bad for Mikka. This was his little sister, and he couldn't protect her because not even he knew what she was capable of.

Mikka and Kilko nodded. Helena was over with Fern, trying to get her up onto a horse. Helena would ride with her, Bondi and Kilko had decided to ride together, and Mikka and I would share another horse. Gregorio would ride on his own.

"Let's move," Helena said as she kicked the horse's side to command it to go.

We rode as fast as we could on the Chero Trail, two horses in front and two in back. The horses not only made the journey faster but also less exhausting since we were no longer on foot. I felt immense relief at no longer having to run.

As we rode, I tried to process what had happened back there. Fern hadn't even known she could do that, and it made me wonder what else she was capable of. A chill ran down my spine. The thought that she somehow possessed that kind of power was frightening. She was still so young, so it couldn't have been easy for her to control whatever she had just done. I thought Mikka was right, we were missing something. The Witch had made Fern immortal but what else could that mean? I hoped that the man in Sutton, Julian, would be able to give us some answers.

Helena and Fern's horse came to a halt at a small opening on the side of the Chero Trail that led to the towns on our right. We had been riding for hours now and had to be close to Sutton.

"Wait here, I'm going to see how far we are," Helena said.

She put Fern on Gregorio's horse so that she could check without putting Fern in additional danger. She then rode off the trail and toward the town.

"How are we going to find Julian when we get to Sutton?" I asked while we waited for Helena's return.

"Well, I think we start with the Sutton Library," Kilko replied.

"Like Helena said, he loved to read. If that was where he used to spend most of his time, then he might be there already." She kept looking around us as she spoke, searching for anything suspicious.

"And if he's not there?" I said.

Kilko raised her eyebrows. "Well, if he's not there, then we figure out what your dream meant and find that place."

I nodded. A backup plan made me feel a lot better about spending all of this time going to Sutton.

Helena came back after just a few minutes. "Commauge," she said with a smile.

That meant we were only an hour away on horseback from Sutton. Relief filled my whole body. We didn't have much more to go.

"Let's ride," Helena said.

Gregorio kept Fern on his horse to save time and we hurried off onto the Chero Trail at full speed with the horses, eager to get to our destination.

We knew we were there because the trail came abruptly to a stop, signaling its end. Helena and the horse she was riding went off first, since she would be our lookout. Her gift could kill, and that meant that anyone she ran into would hopefully fall to the fate of her gift before getting to us. We waited for her to check if the coast was clear and come back.

"I haven't been to the library in Sutton," I said. "I honestly didn't even know they had one." I'd never been beyond the small main street, and hadn't noticed a library of the size and magnitude that Helena had described.

"That's because the library is underground," said Gregorio.

"What?" I said, surprised.

"Yeah, it has a massive amount of historical knowledge held there," Gregorio explained, "so it was built underground to prevent it from ever being destroyed and risking the safety of the historical books that lie within it. Normally you need special access to get into the library, like a pass from a school or a signed letter from the king's court. But since everything is a mess, I'm sure we'll be able to just walk right in." Gregorio seemed excited about the library as he continued, "It was a cool idea for them to build the library like that. It allows the knowledge to get passed down from generation to generation, even if something catastrophic happens." Bondi smiled at his brother's excitement.

No wonder I hadn't ever been there. I wouldn't have been approved.

Helena came back with a smile. "Coast is clear, the city is empty," she said.

"But what does that mean for all the Potens and people that were here before?" I said.

Helena's smile faded. "I'm not sure, but maybe they all fled to the woods or southeast or something," she said.

*Southeast.*

Southeast led to Kinver and the woods below. There was nothing, and I meant nothing, in those woods for much protection. No one could survive there for very long if the whether started to turn. I started to feel sick. I hoped all of those Potens were ok. But I couldn't worry about it now, when we had a job to do. A job that could save them all.

I nodded. We all rode off into Sutton.

# 19

Sutton. It felt like both yesterday and a lifetime ago that Mikka and I were here, trying to pretend we were other people to take the train. It was weird to think about how we were all just strangers then, and now we were family. The thought of sharing such a bond with this incredible group of people made me smile. I hadn't had a family in so long but I knew this was what having one truly meant – they didn't have to be blood-related, all you needed was people that you looked out for and that looked out for you.

We entered Sutton on horseback, slowly trotting into the empty streets. Sutton was, quite literally, a ghost town. There was not a soul to be found here. But unlike the other places we'd seen, it wasn't broken and ransacked. It almost looked like these people had heard what was happening and left before it was too late for them. Hopefully that meant they'd had enough time to get supplies and get out of there before any of them got hurt, and I felt thankful for that thought.

We all followed Helena, since she knew where the library was and who we were looking for.

"Are you sure he'll still be here?"

Mikka said what we were all wondering. If this long trip had been worth it.

"I'm sure," Helena said with conviction. "Especially since the town wasn't attacked, he wouldn't have left." She spoke confidently as she lead us onward, deeper into Sutton.

We moved along small cobblestone paths, past A-frame houses to a large, open field at the other end of town. Of course I'd never been over here before, but from what I could see there was nothing. And I mean *nothing*.

"Well, where's the entrance?" I said.

I knew Gregorio had said it was underground but this was really weird. There wasn't even a sign or anything that would show that the library was here. But Helena dismounted her horse, walked about fifteen steps into the field, bent down to the ground and started knocking.

"What are you doing?" Mikka asked.

Everyone started to get off the horses and Bondi found a nearby tree to tie them to while we all walked over to Helena. She let out a sigh and continued knocking loudly on the ground. Gregorio was smiling as we all watched her – he seemed excited, but I was confused. Helena was just knocking on the earth, and I didn't see an entrance to this place.

Then one loud knock echoed.

"Ah, here we go," Helena said, brushing her hand on the earth. She peeled up the grass to reveal an old, latched wooden door that led into the ground. When she pulled up the handle and opened the door, we could see a dark cobblestone staircase. Strangely, we could see slightly down into the stairwell because the candles that lined the walls were all lit.

"How are the candles still lit?" I said, confused as I peered into the hole in the ground.

"They're willed to stay lit forever," Helena explained. "Potens made this library what it is. It honestly is beautiful, you'll see what I mean."

Bondi caught up to us and Helena led us down the staircase into the library. Gregorio was beaming with excitement.

The staircase was small, only wide enough for one person to fit at a time. We filed in and headed down. I placed my hand on the wall with each step so that I wouldn't fall on Mikka who was in front of me and was surprised to find them warm to the touch. Bondi, who was last, shut the door to the staircase behind us, to not reveal our location. He'd put the horses just far enough away that someone might not think to check here. We just had to hope we would get in, get our answers, and get out quicker than anyone could follow us here.

Since the stairwell and beyond was lit, I could see a tunnel up ahead. It had cobblestone walls and floors leading to a beautiful, ornate wooden door. Helena reached the door first and placed a hand on the wood in a specific spot that was flat. The door's ornate details lit up bright blue for a moment before the door unlatched and slammed open. It was quite alarming.

Helena turned around for a moment. "I have a pass," she said with a smile.

I wondered how she'd gotten a pass to use this library, especially since before we met she'd been hiding in the Zirkels for a while, but it didn't seem like the time to ask. After all, we were on a mission to look for Julian. I was only worried that her access to the library would reveal our location but hopefully, even if it did, we'd be gone by the time anyone got here.

The ornate wooden door opened into a massive library with books filling the walls so far up that you would die if you ever fell from the top shelf. I understood what Helena had meant about the place being beautiful. It had to have every book ever written in here, like a sanctuary for books from all centuries. It smelled like fresh books, old books, pine needles and roasted marshmallows somehow. The walls that didn't have books lining them were made of dark oak, with empty spots revealing cobblestones underneath.

It was an odd look for a library, but I wasn't sure what I'd been expecting considering it was supposed to be underground. Who knew when this thing was built. I just couldn't believe vastness of this place, rows and rows of books in front of us making it look like this room stretched on forever.

I took out my dagger and everyone else grabbed their weapons as well. It was so quiet in here that if there was someone hiding, they would have for sure heard our entrance. Each step on the stone floor made a noise, and there were seven of us.

"Julian?" Helena said aloud. She'd also seemed to realize that there was no point in trying to hide that we were here, we had already made too much noise coming in. "Julian, we're friends of Dova," Helena called. Although it may have been a bad idea to reveal who we were, if we were caught by someone they would know by now anyway.

A loud noise coming from one of the tall book aisles echoed through the massive main room we were in. It sounded like someone had dropped a book from a far height, followed by the sound of someone descending a really tall ladder, each step echoing a little louder. The sound of footsteps filled the room, coming right towards us, although it only sounded like one set of footsteps, slow and inconsistent. We all stood behind Helena and Kilko as they readied their gifts.

Slowly and unsurely, a man emerged from behind the bookshelf. He was short and much older, with white hair. Well, what was left of his hair was white. He was wearing super thick framed glasses and raggedy robes, his left foot slightly dragging behind him as he walked toward us.

"Dova, you say," he said in a low, soft, achy voice. He kept moving closer, and I thought it was because he couldn't see us from that far back. He was squinting, even through the glasses, and stepped just close enough to be within arm's reach. "Julian," he said, slightly bowing his head to say hello. "Pleasure to meet you."

"Yes, Dova was our friend," Helena said. "Julian, we are so glad to have found you."

Julian walked up to her, almost close enough to breathe on her, and pulled up his glasses to get a closer look. "Helena?" he said.

Helena looked surprised. "How... how do you know my name?" she said, stuttering over her words. It was the first time I'd ever heard her stutter.

"Dova told me all about you," Julian said. "All of you. You two must be Gregorio and Bondi. She was right, you do look alike." Helena smiled and Gregorio nodded. "But I'm not sure I know who any of you are?" Julian said when he looked at Mikka, Fern, Kilko and me.

Mikka introduced us. "I'm Mikka. This is my sister, Fern. This is Kilko. And this is my girlfriend, Evergreen."

*Girlfriend.* Mikka said it proudly, even though we hadn't said that out loud before. I felt like I had butterflies.

"Ah, Evergreen," Julian said. "I've heard a lot about you. It's an honor to meet you." He pushed his glasses slightly up his face, like he meant business. "Well, while it really is nice to meet you all, what in the world are you doing here?" He seemed very confused. "You do realize that there is no one left here?" he added.

We all nodded and Helena said, "We were looking for you, actually."

Julian's eyebrows raised, clearly shocked that we were here for him.

"Dova told us a long time ago that you were the person to ask if we didn't have answers to something from the past," she continued.

"Where is Dova?" Julian asked.

My head bowed low to avoid being the one to answer that question.

"She... she passed on," Helena said with a somber expression.

Julian's face went from curious to devasted. He mustered up the question, "How?"

"I'll tell you the whole story," Helena replied. "Where can we talk without being overheard?"

"Come," Julian said. "I'll get you all some tea." He started leading us slowly to a walkway in between two large bookshelves. As we went, he stepped closer to me and said in a low voice, "I'm really sorry about Dova."

"We all are," I answered.

W hat on earth do you mean?" Julian said.

Helena had spent the last ten minutes telling him the whole story, a shortened version of course.

"I mean that not only is the King of Aureum Ignis after us, but the Queen of Melted Cor as well," Helena said. "And we need answers on Fern's immortality and whatever it was that happened to her earlier on the trail." Helena was trying to make sure that the most important parts of the story were Julian's focus. We hadn't told him about the book just yet, but one thing at a time. We needed to know first how to change Fern.

"Ah. Well, it's a lot, I will tell you that." Julian stirred his tea. "This is not what I expected to hear today, that is certain."

We were in a small room that Julian had led us to, somewhere that must have been for the librarians to have their lunch. I wondered where they were and guessed they must have left when they heard about the danger. We were all drinking tea as we sat anxiously waiting for Julian to give us some information. Literally, any information. We had come so far, desperately needing answers, and now we needed them fast.

"Well, I do know a bit about the Tree Witch in question," Julian said, pushing up his glasses again and taking another sip of tea. "I know there is only one Tree Witch left in the entire world at this point, so it had to have been her. She is nameless, as she wants to be. She wouldn't just give someone immortality though, it isn't a hand out. I know that for sure."

It was a lot to take in, and Mikka looked anxious. If the Tree Witch was a monster, then what else had she done to Fern?

"We know that Fern and Mikka's parents traded something with the witch to get Fern back, I said. "It must have also been part of the trade to make her immortal. We don't know what it was though, and that's what we need to find out. We also need to know what Fern's gifts are and how she can channel them because she had no control over what happened earlier." I looked over at Mikka and Fern.

"Hmm. Well, what was it they were after? The king?" Julian said.

In answer, Kilko pulled the Book of Viempro from her bag. Julian stood up and took a step back, his voice suddenly demanding.

"Get. That. Thing. Out. Of. Here."

"Why, what's wrong with it?" Kilko said.

Julian looked like he was in shock. "That book, that awful, vile thing, is cursed. Once you speak its words out loud, you are forever bound to the book. It makes you go mad." Julian spoke with certainty.

"The king and Alco used the book," I said, hopeful that maybe it would have driven them mad too.

"If someone has used that book recently, they will do anything, and I mean *anything*, to try and get it back," Julian said. "People turn on one another after using that book. They will move mountains to get it. If I were you, I'd hide it somewhere that it can never be found, and then I'd take down the king and whoever else has read from it.

Because they will never stop until they find it and read the whole thing aloud. They won't stop until their hearts stop beating."

"If the king read it, then he won't be the one to find it," I said with a grin, "because he still has that cursed gold."

As Kilko slid the book back into her pack, Mikka pushed his way forward, making it clear that he was serious. "Listen, we didn't just come here to get maybes and stories. We need solid answers. How do we fix Fern? Can her immortality be passed to another? What happens to her if it does?"

Julian sighed. "Can I speak freely in front of the little one?" he asked, looking directly at Mikka.

Mikka looked down at Fern and she nodded. "Yeah, sure," Mikka said.

We weren't hiding anything from Fern anymore. There was no point as most of the stuff we needed to know involved her.

"Immortality, like I said, isn't a free pass from the witch," Julian said. "She would have never given that to a human or Potens without a worthy trade. Tree Witches are historically known to be cunning and tricky, so there must have been a hidden trade within it. I have a feeling that if someone tried to just take the immortality, they wouldn't be able to. I feel like there's some sort of long-term deal, like maybe Fern is tethered to the witch in some way. No one would be able to just take whatever Fern has been given." Julian's voice got quieter. "My suggestion would be to hide the book, to find the witch, and to hide from the king and queen until they realize that they cannot win or find the items."

I could tell from the way Julian said those words that he knew we wouldn't be able to hide from them.

"So let me get this straight, you don't think anyone could even take her immortality?" Mikka said with obvious relief.

Julian didn't look as hopeful as Mikka did. "No, what I'm saying is that if it was a trade, the witch wouldn't just allow it to be given up. There's something more here that you must find out from the witch."

"Where do we find this last Tree Witch?" I said, looking around at the others. It seemed like no one knew exactly where to find her, they were all shaking their heads.

"In Kinver," Julian said without hesitation. "She lives in the deep woods of Kinver."

Right back to where this all started. My home.

*My dream.* I looked at Mikka while he looked right at me. We both knew that going back to Kinver would be related to my path-dream that had happened in the Sunken Forest.

"How do we find her?" Bondi asked.

I couldn't imagine having to find this witch, or what it would mean if we did find her. The idea of having to intentionally go looking for this awful creature, when all we'd been doing was trying to run away from horrible monsters, was exhausting to think about. Especially when I'd just had a dream that I was in that forest. The darkness in that dream still sent a chill down my spine.

"Tree Witches usually don't leave their dens other than to hunt, or so I've read," Julian said. "But they do love fresh orange peels and wine. The witch will probably come out if you bring those into the forest and ask for her. The only problem is you need to have some-thing big you'd be willing to trade. If she doesn't like the trade, she's bound to kill you." That sounded promising. "The other thing is that she hasn't been sighted in a while," Julian added. "I know she's still out there, and that the last she was seen was in the forests outside of Kinver, but that was a few years ago." She must have been seen when she found Fern all those years ago.     Great. This wasn't as helpful as we had hoped. We now knew that no one could take Fern's immortality, but who would believe that? We'd also found out that something tied the witch with Fern, but that made all this worse because the uncertainty and not knowing what that meant was terrifying. I felt frustrated that we had come all this way for a bunch of maybes and more questions.

"What do you suggest we do with the book?" Helena said impatiently. I knew she also felt frustrated that we hadn't gotten the answers we needed here.

"Hide it somewhere in Kinver," Julian said. "It is crucial that you hide it before you go into the center of the forest to see the witch. If you go to her with it, she will sense that it's there, and if she knows that it's there, it's the only thing she'll accept for a trade." Julian then added, "I can't know where you hide it. I can't risk my life over that information."

He was right. If we told him, he could be tortured into telling someone else where it was. The only way we could ensure that the book was safely away from others was to never tell anyone about where we put it.

"What should we trade?" I asked.

Julian shook his head. "It must be something of worth. She could take a few years off your life, or part of your gift, or a service of some sort. Whatever you decide, make sure that you listen to the entire trade. She's tricky, and she'll try to get more than she's asking for."

"Thank you for the information, Julian," I said. "Are you just going to stay here? Do you want to come with us?" Even though the answers weren't everything we needed, they had gotten us heading in the right direction.

"I can't leave my books," he said calmly. "I will stay here with them, die with them someday."

"Well, we have to get going," I said. "Thank you, for everything. And I'm really sorry about Dova." I knew that they had been friends long before we had met.

He nodded. "Me too," he said.

Julian happened to have oranges that we could peel for the witch, and he also had wine in the library. He gave both to us so that we could try and lure her out when we reached the Sunken Forest.

We said our goodbyes and headed out the way we'd come in. Gregorio was still looking around in awe as we left, and I think he would have stayed here if he had the option. We walked back through the grand hall of the library, back up the cobblestone staircase and back out of the small door that led us out of the underground back to the open earth above us. I half-expected to open the door and find the King's Guard, but thankfully there was no one else around, just silence. That was a huge relief, and I felt like I could breathe again, knowing that we weren't walking back into a trap. Thankfully the horses were still there too. They were slightly tucked away, but we could see them from here as we closed the door and put some grass and leaves back on to cover it.

As we walked over to the horses, I wondered if the king or queen had survived the water. I knew that since the King's Guard had found us it meant they probably had, but I also wanted to hope that they didn't. A big part of me would feel relief if they hadn't made it, but I felt in my gut that they were still alive. I had to push that aside though, because it didn't matter right now. We had something to do that was more important and that required our immediate attention.

*Kinver.*

We were going to Kinver. It felt weird to even think about going back to Kinver. From the moment I'd left, I didn't think I would ever get a chance to go back there. We had to hide the book before finding the witch, but in order to get to Kinver we needed to go through the edge of the Sunken Forest first. We needed to be as far from the center where the witch lived while we still had the book.

This was the forest I loved. The forest I knew so well. The forest that had healed me and given me my love for spending time outside. The forest where I was certain something would go wrong because of my dream. We didn't have a choice though. We had to find the witch.

"Where are we going to hide the book?" Mikka said while Bondi and Gregorio readied the horses. Fern stood quietly, leaning slightly against a tree, while Helena and Kilko were chatting about some old memory that had them smiling.

"I'm not quite sure," I replied as I tried to think of what Kinver used to be, what places there were to hide things. It needed to be somewhere no one would be able to find but us, at least for a little while.

"We could dig a hole in Kinver and hide it somewhere random?" Helena said, but her voice trailed off as she realized that it wasn't the strongest of ideas.

"I think the soil being lifted up and changed would give it away," I said, trying not to hurt Helena's feelings. "Plus, if they find us without the book they're going to think to look in Kinver. We need to think more out-of-the-box."

I kept thinking of different places in the town. The little shops that lined downtown didn't have many good long-term hiding spots. I mean sure, there were plenty of places we could put it for now, but the problem would be they weren't long-term places to hide it. Someone would stumble on the book eventually, and if it fell into someone else's hands, that would be an absolute disaster. Where could we put it that would make it hard to find but didn't need to be long-term?

Then it hit me. "The well," I said.

Everyone looked around at one another and Mikka said, "The well? The one at the edge of Kinver? The book might float."

I shook my head. "Not if we tied a rock to it and sunk it deep within the well. I could create a tea that we could dump down there, with a smell that would make people forget anything they saw. I've made forgetful-draughts before. It would buy us time to find the witch and then we could come back, get the book, and find somewhere better to put it." I finished with a grin.

"Wouldn't people have to drink the water for the forgetful-draught to work though?" Mikka said.

I looked around at everyone with a smug expression. "Well... " My voice trailed off because I hadn't really wanted to share what I was about to say. Before all this, even talking about it would have gotten me in trouble. But there was no one to get me in trouble here. "Um, you see, there's a way to make it powerful enough that you'd only have to smell it. Which would mean anyone who leaned over would immediately forget what they saw." I wasn't supposed to use that kind of gift and brewing combination. It was the law that you couldn't purposefully poison someone in that way.

Mikka's eyes had widened and he was shaking his head, impressed. Gregorio and Bondi smiled. Fern still stood with her back to the tree.

"That's an awesome idea," Kilko said.

Helena raised her eyebrows and nodded in agreement as Bondi asked, "Where are we going to get the stuff for you to make the tea though?"

I smiled. "My shop, of course."

## 21

The King

The king sat on his throne. He was exhausted. Getting out of the ocean alive had been a miracle, but what had happened after was even better.

He'd made a deal with the queen. He'd known that it was the only way to survive, and unfortunately for the queen, he'd found out her secret once he'd boarded her ship. The thought made him smile, his grin stretching from ear to ear. He had outwitted her, and there was no way she could know. She'd left that deal thinking she was the one with the better end of it, but it was actually him that had walked away with the advantage.

The queen was playing her part for now: she would find Fern and the book. Meanwhile, the king had no intention of following through on his end of the deal, and once the queen had completed her task, he could get rid of her. With the false information he had given her, the rest of that group of thieves would soon be dead, and all that would be left would be Fern and the Book of Viempro. All that was needed until then was time.

A man in armor entered the room. "We got confirmation that the group is headed to Kinver, just like she said they would."

He had outsmarted them. He had outsmarted them all. With the power of the gold still stopping him from getting what he wanted, he did still have to do things through Alco. So, he was trusting Alco to make the right decisions, for now.

The king nodded to the man. "Good, good. Update me when it's all over." He put his feet up on the foot rest and laid back.

The guard nodded and rushed away from the king as if he now feared him, as if he now saw something dark. A grin filled the king's face as he sunk deeper into his throne.

He knew he had won.

The sun had set and risen two times since we'd left the library. We had all been riding the horses so we were more alert and less tired as we moved. We did have to stop every few hours to feed them and give them time to rest too, but we needed to put as much distance between us and that library as possible. We did stop for a few hours to sleep each day when everyone got too tired to even sit up on the horses. The horses were part of the king's army, which meant they were well-trained and in shape to be riding like this, although we still felt like we needed to give them little breaks. Who knew when we would need to escape something again? We needed them to be strong and ready.

After a just a few more hours, we would be getting close to Kinver. We brought the horses from a gallop to a trot so that we could eat and discuss our plan while we rode. Kilko unzipped a bag as we slowly trotted along on the horses and handed out little snacks to everyone, making sure Fern got them first. Fern smiled as she grabbed a small orange to peel and eat. She would discard the peels in the pack for later, as we would need them for the witch.

"The well should keep the book hidden for long enough that we'll be able to go find the witch," Mikka said, "but we need to figure out what to trade with her."

I nodded while Helena looked like she was deep in thought, trying to figure out something worthy to trade that wouldn't get one of us killed. I couldn't think of anything worthwhile except someone's gift, and mine wasn't even worth trading. I pondered the thought for a moment, waiting for inspiration to hit me. We were headed through the forest to Kinver, farther south that I had ever been. We'd had to bypass the Ridge so that we could keep the horses. It was a longer journey, but it made more sense to go around.

"What if we gave up our weapons?" Bondi said.

Helena shook her head. "The Tree Witch is the last of her kind. She'll be smart and have a lot of resources. Weapons aren't going to be something she wants to trade." She was keeping her head on a swivel, not only to make sure no one was following us but also that we weren't running into anyone that could overhear this conversation.

"She'll want someone's gift," Kilko said.

A chill went down my spine. No one was going to give their gift up for this, and Bondi already knew what that was like. He was looking off to the side, also deep thought. I knew in my heart that he wished he had his gift still as an option for something to give, but we weren't even sure it was possible to get a gift back. A part of him might always be missing.

I tried to change the subject so he wouldn't think about it. "What if we gave her my golden dagger?" I said. "It has that special gold, so it's different than a regular weapon."

Helena shrugged and said, "Maybe, but I don't think she would want a weapon. Like I said, she's going to be smart, she's going to try and trick us. Although maybe she might want it if we were able to make it seem more enticing."

But I couldn't make the dagger more exciting, and I didn't have anything else to offer that was of more value, other than my life. Everyone paused in thought for a moment, but it was hard to concentrate because all I could hear were people chewing their snacks and the sound of the horses' hooves on the forest floor. It was distracting.

"There would be bad consequences for not showing up with the right type of thing," Helena said after the long silence. "We have to think of something that would be valuable but that couldn't be interpreted wrongly. We don't want her tricking us into making a deal we can't back out of. We can't lose someone's life to this."

We all nodded as we tried to think of something good that we could offer the witch. It was hard to think of anything important enough that would be worth something but would also not take away something we desperately needed. It had to be the perfect combination of valuable and something we could lose.

"What about if we traded a service?" Kilko said.

I raised my eyebrows. "What kind of service?" I said in anticipation. I realized that this could be a good option, since it would be something we could do without sacrificing something big, like our lives.

Bondi looked at Kilko and said, "A service is not a bad idea, but I think we'd have to be smart with it. What could we give that wouldn't take us too much time?" He was being the voice of reason – we couldn't go off on another long mission.

"What if... " Kilko's voice trailed off for a moment as she thought about Bondi's words. Then she said, "What if we traded her one service, so if she wanted something done we could send a few of us to do it, and then we'd get what we need in return?"

It wasn't a bad idea except the witch was known to be tricky, so we would have to know specifically what she was asking for.

"What if she wants us to kill someone for her though?" Mikka asked. "Or what if it's something that's really far away? We can't risk sending a few of us off to complete the trade without getting our answers."

We all looked around at each other but it was Kilko who said, "It is possible that she will ask us to kill someone. But we have to do something, so I think it's worth the risk. Especially since, if we don't get the answers to our questions, the fate of the entire world as we know it is at risk. And we could also tell her that we need the answers first, so if we don't finish the service she's asking for, then she can have one of our gifts."

Mikka raised his eyebrows. It was a terrifying trade, but one that would give us the answers we needed. And as long as we followed through with the deal, it wouldn't cause harm to any of our friends. I knew in my heart that it was a risk to try and trade something with the Tree Witch but I also knew that we were running out of time and options. We couldn't end up with one of us dead, so we did need a better trade.

"Even if she wanted us to kill someone, we would have to be specific about the details and why she wanted that service," I said. "Since we know that she's tricky, we must take our time to understand what she wants first, before agreeing to any bargain. We might be able to find out a way to get out of following through with it if needed." I smiled.

"What do you mean?" Mikka said.

"I told you, I'm good at brewing forgetful-draughts," I said with a smirk. We could make the witch forget the bargain after she'd told us what we needed. Then we would have enough time to escape and figure out what our next steps were.

Everyone smiled except Helena. "The only thing is we don't know what kind of power she possesses. Your forgetful-draught might not work on her," she said solemnly.

"Well, I think it might be our only option that sounds like it would work," Kilko said, "and I think it's worth the risk of not knowing what she can do. I think we plan for that for now, and if someone has a better idea, we can figure out the details as we go."

Helena shrugged and nodded. It was a plan, for the moment at least.

We gave the horses some water and some of our snacks to keep them happy and healthy, but we couldn't rest for too long. Once they were fed, we kept moving. We had to pick up our pace as we were trying to get to Kinver before nightfall. At least it took much less time on horseback than it had when Mikka and I first ran through this forest months and months ago to get to Sutton. We continued to head south, avoiding the Ridge, and then rode swiftly east towards Kinver.

I wrapped my arms tightly around Mikka as we rode, worried about what would happen if I let go. I felt this impending doom within that made me wonder if we would ever get out of this mess. But I had to hold on to hope. We had all been so close to being captured so many times that I didn't want to let go of Mikka for even a moment. I was afraid that we might never get this again. I squeezed him tighter.

The sun was starting to set now. But we were close, so close. I could feel it. I recognized these trees, these woods that were my own. I had spent so much time in these forests, spent so much time learning the creatures that lived here, the ecosystems, how to survive on my own. It felt like home being in this space.

But this time, my home felt dark. I knew that my dream would happen here, which made every step in the forest a step closer to potential death.

"Stop here," I said. Everyone slowed their pace to a walk and then pulled the horses to a stop.

"Why here?" Gregorio said, looking around at the empty forest.

"We're about a mile from Kinver," I said. "We should tie the horses up soon, so they won't be seen. We'll need to be on foot in the town so we can sneak around without causing alarm."

"How do you know?" Gregorio said.

"These are my woods," I told him. "I've spent more time in here than anywhere else on my own. I know these trees better than I even know myself."

Gregorio smiled, and I could see Mikka nod from in front of me as he brought our horse to a stop. I squeezed him tighter, trying to make the moment last just a second longer before we would have to head out into more danger.

We all got off the horses and Gregorio tied them to a tree. Bondi put out a small jug of water and some food for them to nibble on while we were gone. I was thankful that we'd been able to use the horses because without them, we would probably still be on the Chero Trail, not even at the library yet. They'd cut our time in half for this journey, and time was all we had to keep ourselves away from danger.

I petted the mane of the horse that we'd ridden and said, "Thank you," even though I knew that it wouldn't respond.

Fern was also petting one of the other horses. She didn't say any-thing, but she looked sad to leave it. Her entire life had changed so much since she was taken from her family, from Mikka. I knew what it felt like to lose everyone you loved, so I touched her shoulder to let her know I was here. Not just physically next to her, but here for her. She looked up at me and smiled. We didn't need to share words to express that she and I were the same.

I walked over to the group as they readied their weapons into easy access places, ready for where we would be headed. "Alright, here's the plan," I said out loud to everyone while they gathered their stuff. "We go into Kinver and immediately split up into two groups. One group goes to look for supplies, literally anything we could use – weapons, food, safety kits, anything. The other group will go to my shop and then dump the book in the well. We'll have to split up to save time, every second counts now. Mikka, Kilko and I will go to stash the book while Fern, Gregorio, Helena and Bondi go and get extra supplies." Mikka looked at me with a worried expression but I told him, "We have to keep Fern separate from the book. And Helena will keep her safe."

I said it not as a question but as a fact. Helena had the most powerful gift out of anyone, and she would not let Fern be harmed. We also needed to split up Kilko and Helena because both of them could protect us by knocking out or killing a bunch of people at once.

Helena nodded and grabbed Fern's hand in hers. Fern smiled, and each group grabbed a pack. We took a potion from the pack that we'd carried them all in and put it into the other pack, just in case. The potion was labeled with a skull and crossbones, and underneath the drawing were the words 'Throw at Enemies.' We had no idea what it did, but it could come in handy.

Fern stayed quiet as we got ready to go. She was always looking around, taking everything in, but she wouldn't communicate that much with anyone but Mikka. She seemed to like Helena though, and Helena would not let any harm come to her – Helena would die before allowing that to happen. Not only that, but Fern also had a gift that we couldn't explain, and I think that if she were in harm's way again, she'd someone muster up the courage to use it.

"Helena, keep her safe," Mikka said. He touched Fern's head and told her, "You be brave now, ok?" Fern smiled, nodded and gave him a hug, still staying quiet as she did so.

We had to do this right. There was no time for mistakes now, no time for things to go wrong. We were running out of time before the king or queen might find us, and we couldn't let them do that while we still had the book. We needed that leverage in order to stay alive.

"Let's do this," Kilko said.

We were taking Kilko with us because she would be able to cause a distraction if we needed one. Putting people to sleep would cause them no harm, but it would allow us to get what we needed to accomplish done and get out of there before anyone woke up. The last thing I wanted was for any harm to come to anyone that had remained in Kinver, so we had to hope that any people we ran into would walk the other way. The majority of our group though were going after the supplies, since they would need more hands to hold stuff. We would need as many extra weapons as they could find around town, so that we'd have options for the witch if she didn't take our bargain.

Helena, Bondi, Gregorio and Fern went east along the forest, and would enter into Kinver from that direction. We waved as they ran off along the outskirts of the woods. We, meanwhile, were right where we needed to be, close to my shop.

Mikka peeked through the trees at the streets of Kinver, to see if there was anyone out there. "I don't see anyone," he said.

I nodded. "What is weird is that all these towns are empty. Where are all the people?" I asked.

Kilko looked at me. "Hiding. They're all hiding. Maybe in the woods, maybe in the basements of their own houses. They're here, we just can't see them. That I'm sure of. I can feel them here."

I didn't quite understand how she knew that, but I was going to trust her on it. We had nothing but trust in each other right now, and that was all we could hold onto until we somehow got out of this mess.

We listened for any sound, any movement that may let us know we should wait. If there were people here, they may report us if it meant ensuring their own safety, so we had to be quiet, as quiet as we could.

But there was just silence.

"My shop is just over there," I whispered. "There's a door that we can use to access it from that back alleyway. Let's go."

Kilko and Mikka both nodded, and the three of us hurried out of the woods into the town. The small alley that I remembered so well was just a hundred yards away. It was so quiet around us that even our soft footsteps were making quite a bit of noise. We were trying to avoid that but we had no choice, we had to keep moving. The only way to make less noise was to move more slowly, but we didn't have time to waste.

"This way," I whispered, gesturing for us to move. We hurried quickly towards the alley that I knew so well. When I'd left Kinver I hadn't been sure that I'd ever see this place again, so it felt nostalgic to be here. It brought back a lot of feelings.

The alley was wider than most, providing lots of room for moonlight to shine through from above and illuminate our surroundings. The back door to my shop was still covered in vines – I'd always had a way with plants, and had been able to nurture these to grow over the door. It had looked so pretty once, but now most of the vines were dead and brown. The sight of them made me quite sad, since I knew that they were dying because I wasn't there to tend to them. They covered a very small, deep-oak door, which was held on by nothing more than a small latch. I touched the door softly, trying to let the vines know that I was sorry.

I'd never had much to hide here, never had much to protect. I'd also never had a lot of money for repairs, and the tea itself was useless without a Potens to will it to life, so there was never any need for much security. There'd never been much to worry about in Kinver until a while ago, it had always been fairly safe. I wished now that I had prepared for everything that had happened since I'd left, but who could have known? There wasn't time for would haves, could haves, should haves.

I slid the latch open to unhook the door, peering around it to find that my always-messy back room had been completely ransacked. The walls, which were painted a deep purple, were the only thing still intact. All of my shelves, my upcycled jars, my containers of various types of tea were all completely shattered. The tea leaves were sprawled out on the floor, all mixed and unsorted.

I wanted to scream or cry, but in comparison with everything we'd been through and all that we'd lost already, this didn't seem nearly as bad. I'd never expected to see this place again, so even though it was breaking my heart to see it in this shape, I was relieved to be back inside the shop that I had worked so hard for. It smelled strongly of lavender and cloves from the broken vases and jars.

It had taken me years and years to find all of these different tea leaves, and now that they were all scattered on the floor, I would never be able to correctly sort them out. Not that I needed to, we weren't planning on staying here and starting over. That was completely out of the question. But it still crossed my mind, even though for now I had to focus and pay attention to what I needed to find in this moment. There wasn't time to mourn the tea shop right now, I could worry about that later. Plus, if we didn't defeat the king and queen, there would be no tea shop left to even fix up in the future.

I wanted to make a forgetful-draught, but a regular one just wouldn't do. The typical forgetful-draughts only lasted for a short while, and you had to drink them for them to be effective, which wouldn't work since the tea would be in the well. I needed to make the tea effective by smell, but that would involve a combination that I would usually never use on a person because it was considered illegal. Potens weren't allowed to purposefully harm humans, under penalty of death, and this would technically harm anyone that used it. The recipe was in a banned book about out-of-bounds teas that were no longer allowed to be made, although I'd only been reading it so that I wouldn't accidently try and combine things that ended up being poisonous, or even deadly.

I dug through the drawers to see if I had any of the pre-made capsules of the regular tea, since forgetful-draughts had been one of the most popular teas that I brewed back when I worked here. I quietly rummaged through drawer after drawer but found no capsules. This would take longer without them, and then I would need to combine the ingredients with something else in order to make the tea more powerful.

"Can we help?" Kilko whispered.

"Yes, we're looking for small yellow capsules that have crushed up leaves in them," I said. I paused for a moment to think of what we could find if the capsules were missing or had been stolen, and then said, "If you can't find them, look for a small jar, no larger than a candle, with a lid. It will have a blue cap and a green powder in it."

I looked at Kilko and Mikka. We did need one more thing, but it was a powder I wasn't supposed to have in the first place. It was an enrichment powder that I'd made a while back, just to see if I could. I was a little embarrassed to tell them about it, but we all needed to look if we were going to get out of here in time.

"Uh, I also need to find a small vile of purple powder," I said as I looked at my friends. "It should be tied to a necklace. It's an enrichment powder."

Kilko raised an eyebrow, obviously knowing not only that the purpose of the powder was to increase the effects of any normal tea to something extreme, but also the dangers of such a powder. She just shrugged though and walked carefully into the front end of my shop, the customer-facing side, to continue the search. She was trying not to step on all of the broken glass, not only to not get hurt but to avoid making any noise.

Mikka, however, stayed in the back with me, looking patiently for the things I had mentioned while I opened each drawer. Some of the broken drawers had always broken, because I hadn't had the money to fix them, and some of the drawers were missing entirely from whoever had searched this place. I could hear Kilko continuing to open drawers in the front of the shop too. We were making too much noise, but we didn't have the time to search more quietly.

"I found it," Mikka said in a whisper loud enough for Kilko to hear from the front.

Kilko came rushing back in with the small purple vile in her hand. "Got it!" she said with a smile.

I looked over at Mikka and in his hand was the very small jar of forgetful powder. I anxiously took it from his hands before reaching over to Kilko and placing the necklace of purple enrichment powder around my neck.

"One more thing we need to find, this one should be easy," I said. "I need a large match. I had boxes and boxes of them."

"I saw a box of matches in the front, I'll go grab them," Kilko said.

I nodded as she darted over to rummage through the broken things on the floor in the front. She came back within sixty seconds holding the box of matches, and I grabbed those too. We were ready to go.

"Let's hide this thing," I said. Kilko and Mikka both nodded. We'd need to hurry. The more time we took, the more opportunity others had to catch up with us.

We quietly went back out the exit, running down the alley and behind the backs of the shops to stay hidden as we headed to the well. The well was at the far end of town, out of sight from the small main street of Kinver. As we hurried past the broken back doors of all of the little shops, I tried not to get worked up over what Kinver had become. A ghost town.

Near the end of main street was a small cobblestone path that led to the edge of the woods. There was the well, surrounded by a knee-high wall made of large, mismatched stones. The well itself had been there for centuries, and the wood that held up the small cover to protect it from the elements was aged and brittle.

"Grab a heavy stone and the rope," I said to Mikka and Kilko. Mikka darted behind the well to grab the perfect-sized stone while Kilko grabbed a rope that she had stored in her backpack.

I started to pull up the bucket from the inside of the well to get water for the tea I would make. It took several heavy pulls to get the bucket up with enough water to poison the whole well, and as I pulled the heavy wooden bucket out I spilled some water onto the cobblestones. Luckily I had enough to continue without having to redraw the water, so I sat down, readying myself to create the powerful forgetful-draught. Mikka had meanwhile come back with the stone, and both he and Kilko worked together to tie the book securely to a rock. They then tied the rope to the side of the bucket I was using so it couldn't be seen from the top, and took up positions to keep watch and make sure no one had followed us here.

"Once I make this, both of you must step back, otherwise this stuff will make you forget too," I said. "I'm going to end up having the effects of the tea on me, which means you'll have to deal with me having completely forgotten where I am or who I am for a little while."

Mikka looked upset at this but nodded, even though he didn't like the idea. He didn't want to see me disoriented, and knew it would be hard to convince my confused self to go with them. I looked up at him though and nodded to show that I would be ok.

"Here goes nothing," I said.

I didn't need to heat the tea for this brew. The powder would dissolve into the water and I could add my gift to will it to work with a match. I wanted the tea to be extra potent, since it would need to be effective even if someone just leaned their head over the well, so I poured the entire tiny jar of green powder into the bucket. I then pulled off the necklace containing the purple enrichment powder, which glimmered and swirled inside the little vile. I pulled the tiny cork out and dumped the contents into the water, mixing everything together.

It started to bubble as it reacted, so I placed my hands firmly around the bucket and started to will the powder to work. The air smelled nice from the compound of the powders mixing into the water, and the water swirled in bright colors once the bubbling stopped. All I had left to do was to use the match to make it strong and able to be effective just by scent (totally illegal).

I took one large match out of the box and lit it. Holding it in my hands, I willed the entire match to ignite, not just the top. I was changing the properties of the match to make this tea the strongest forgetful-draught there'd ever been. The match burst into purple flames as it touched the water, the entire bucket bursting into those flames for just a moment before it went back to normal. It looked like regular water again, even though this was about to be the most powerful tea ever brewed.

I gestured for Kilko and Mikka to back up some more so they wouldn't be affected by it. Then, I grabbed the heavy bucket and stood up. It wasn't quite done yet though, I still had to will it all together. I set the bucket, book and rock on the side of the well, so they would all fall in at the same time. Finally, I placed both of my hands on either side of the bucket, closed my eyes and willed the ingredients together. The water swirled in purple and golden streaks as I willed it, making it fully powerful. Before I could forget, I pushed the rock and book off into the well, watching the bucket get pulled in after them.

The fumes made my head spin. I took a step back and everything went black.

When I awoke, I was really confused as to where I was. I was alone in the Forest. Where had all of my friends gone?

"Mikka? Kilko?" I said loudly, but no one answered.

I knew this place. I'd been here before. I sat up and frantically looked around. I tried to start walking forward but felt stuck. The darkness was enveloping me from behind. The hairs on my arms started to stand up and I got the chills. I turned around to see what it was and the figure was there. The figure that the darkness was coming from. I tried to scream but it felt like no sound came out. The darkness was deafening. I felt cold and couldn't see. I could just feel it getting closer, closer and closer...

"Ever!" Mikka shouted as he shook me.

He was shouting like it didn't matter how loud he was being. I blinked open my eyes to look at him.

"You're dreaming again," he said.

I looked around to see everyone in our group. My heart was pounding. I was not alone, thank the heavens.

"What... what happened?" I said as I tried to get up.

Mikka handed me some water. "You passed out when you smelled the forgetful-draught," he said. "We didn't think that would happen, but I think you used so much of your gift that your body just gave out. We were thinking it would be for just a moment, but you weren't waking up so we carried you into the forest to our meeting spot. The rest of the group was already here with the supplies and weapons. I was worried that you'd made the tea wrong and that you'd never wake back up, but then you started shouting, like a nightmare. And now you're here. You're awake." He said the last part as if he was trying to convince himself that I was actually awake and ok.

I didn't remember passing out. "I was back in that nightmare," I explained. "That path-dream. I was alone, here in this forest, and there was a figure that was creating some sort of darkness. I can't really describe what they looked like because before they got too close, I woke up." I took a sip of water. "I think that whatever this dream is, it will happen soon. I can feel it."

Mikka shook his head in disagreement. "You won't ever be alone here," he said. "So no, it won't happen like that." He brushed my hair out of my face.

In my last path-dream, I hadn't known Dova was going to be there until it happened, so it was possible that I wouldn't be alone when this new dream happened either.

"What did we get?" I said, looking at the group that had gone out for supplies.

Bondi looked excited to show me. He pulled out three large swords and laid them on the ground. They were all white gold, which meant they were expensive and had been made custom for someone with a lot of money, probably someone that was friends with the king. He then pulled out an axe – not a golden one, but a copper-looking one.

I knew that was for me. I felt comfortable with an axe, and felt naked without my golden one. The dagger helped, but I missed my family heirloom. I looked at Bondi with smiling eyes and nodded. He smiled and nodded back.

"We had to use that potion on a few King's Guard," Gregorio said with a solemn tone. "We threw it just like the bottle said. We thought it had just knocked them out, but I don't think they made it." Gregorio had started pulling out a bunch of dried food and first aid supplies that he'd found, while Helena pulled out two bows. A big bag of arrows were strapped to her back.

"Well done," I said.

But Helena shook her head. "No, YOU well done," she said with a smile. "I'm sorry I underestimated your gift. It's remarkable what you were able to do with that forgetful-draught. Mikka and Kilko told us all about how you made it. It's pretty incredible."

I felt so seen. No one ever cared for my gift, and a compliment coming from Helena meant the world to me. I nodded and smiled, not having anything to say.

"We need to get going," Mikka said. "We're going to run out of time, and we need to find the witch before someone else finds us first."

We all looked at each other and nodded in agreement before packing up our backpacks and getting back on the horses.

It was time to find the witch.

23

We discussed who would be the best fit to talk to the witch and all agreed that Helena seemed like the best option. She had a gift like no other, and she had an easier time masking her emotions. She was brave, that was certain, and she had a stern look to her face that would show the witch we meant business.

Kilko would have also been a good option, since she had a vast knowledge of things and could speak clearly without a shaky voice. And I knew for certain it shouldn't be me. I'd crack under the pressure and have a panic attack. But hey, everyone has their strong suits, and speaking for our lives for sure was not mine.

Not only was Helena strong and able to defend us if we needed her to, the witch would also probably be able to sense her powers which meant that she would fear her too. We were truly risking our lives going to find the witch and we couldn't die because I had a hard time holding a straight face and wouldn't stop shaking with anxiety. Helena was the best option. I repeated that to myself, even though I wanted to be brave in this moment.

"What will she look like?" I asked, anxious to know what we

would be facing and trying to distract my thoughts. The noise of the horses trotting filled the looming silence as everyone seemed to be eagerly waiting for the answer to my question. After everything we'd been through, it seemed hard to imagine something more terrifying that the things we'd already seen.

Helena looked up. "I'm not entirely sure," she said, "but legend says witches are more similar to monsters than people. But who knows, most people are fortunate enough to never run into one."

I watched Helena as she kept her gaze forward, like she was trying to distract herself from what she would need to do soon. My own mind raced. I couldn't picture what the witch might look like, but I was certain I didn't want to find out. But we were going to, and that path-dream crept into my mind again, and the darkness that surrounded it. I had to find out more.

"Fern, do you remember?" I asked as I looked at Mikka's little sister. It seemed like everyone held their breath, almost hoping she may have some memory to give us a leg-up.

But she shook her head quickly. "No, I don't even remember meeting her," Fern said.

Disappointment filled me, but also a sense of relief, because I was happy to know that she didn't remember that awful encounter. But I'd also hoped that she did so we would know what we were up against.

"Where exactly are we going?" Mikka said to Helena and Kilko, who were leading us on the horses. We were heading deeper into the woods with the orange peels and the wine, ready to lure the witch out into our space.

It was hard to completely distinguish where we were, but this did all look familiar to me. Just like in my path-dream. I didn't really understand how Helena and Kilko knew where to go, but it did feel like there was a pull to go this way, like my heart knew that this was the right path. Even though my head was screaming to run the other way.

"Just a little longer and we'll be at the heart of this forest," Helena said. "Once we get there, I have a plan on what we can do to lure her in."

Mikka nodded, understanding that we wouldn't need to know how Helena planned to do it because we would see it all unfold in a few moments.

"How do we even know she's here?" I said.

Kilko and Helena looked at each other before turning around to look at me and Mikka on the horse. "Well, we wouldn't have known for sure before, but your path-dream shows that she'll be here," Helena said.

"The dark figure? You for sure think that was her?" I said, trying to stay calm.

They didn't need to say anything though, I had already known. My heart was beating out of my chest, and I could feel a panic attack coming on. I knew that this felt like the last time I'd had that path-dream. I didn't know then that it was something that would absolutely happen, and I'd hoped I might be wrong about this one. Although I wanted to find the witch, something in my gut made me feel absolutely terrified. Something felt wrong. The last time one of these path-dreams had come true, Dova died.

Mikka must have sensed that something was wrong. He placed one of his hands over the hand that I had wrapped around his waist, holding on to him in front of me. I squeezed his hand with my thumb, trying to thank him for knowing that I was feeling anxious without making everyone else aware of it. Although I had been able to push through most things with my anxiety, I didn't want the others to know because I didn't want anyone to think I was afraid. I would do this, even with my anxiety still there, lurking under the surface.

My head started to spin, but I knew I had someone here that would provide me with comfort if it got too bad. I squeezed Mikka's hand again while I practiced deep breathing quietly and tried to calm my heart down. I noticed that this part of the woods was looking more and more familiar, and I knew what that meant. We were close, very close to where my dream occurred. My anxiety turned into terror even as I was trying to calm myself down. I couldn't be dealing with a panic attack right now, there was no time for people to be worrying about me.

I squeezed Mikka's hand harder and closed my eyes as I continued to breathe deeply. Inhale, exhale. Inhale, exhale. I tried to count my breaths as Mikka's hand pressed tightly on mine. My breathing started to steady and my heart rate started to slowly come back to normal. I began to feel a little better. Not perfect, but better. I could deal with better. It felt like this massive weight was starting to lift off of my chest, like things were starting to slow back down. I'd been able to stop this panic attack before it got too overwhelming, and I realized that I'd gotten better at working through my anxiety in these situations.

Helena stopped abruptly. We all came to a halt, following her lead. We'd gone over the plan so many times and had discussed backup plans too for if things didn't go as planned. But even though I felt prepared to play my part, I knew it didn't matter if the witch decided to give us her worst. This was ancient magic, and she probably had more power than we could ever imagine. I knew that even if we were as prepared as we could be, we couldn't predict what would happen if the witch decided to take us all out.

She was more powerful than any gifted person, even more powerful than Dova. I missed Dova and the comfort she'd provided. I took a deep breath at the thought of her and looked up through the trees, to acknowledge that I was thinking of her. There was a small window of light that was peeking through the trees, and I knew that it had to be her looking down on us, ensuring that we would be alright.

We all got off our horses at Helena's request. Kilko took the small glass-corked bottle of wine out of her pack while Helena grabbed the netted bag that contained the orange peels from earlier. It smelled so strongly of citrus from where I was standing that if this was the way to lure the Tree Witch, she would have no choice but to come.

I felt a shiver run down my spine and I looked around quickly, trying to see if the darkness was coming. But nothing was there. I closed my eyes for a moment to take a deep breath, trying to ground myself on the earth beneath me, but it was hard with this much at stake. As I did, everyone else stood looking at Helena, listening to any small sound around us to see if my path-dream would come true.

Helena's voice shattered the silence as she spoke into the emptiness of the deep woods. "We summon you, great Tree Witch," she called. "We call you forth to strike a bargain." The sound of Helena's voice echoed off of the trees, as if even the trees were telling us that there was no life around here.

The normal forest sounds of this space completely disappeared. It felt like all of the creatures were hiding from the witch, which made me think we should maybe be hiding too. The stillness was eerie. There wasn't even the chirp of a bird, nor the sound of a cricket, nor the rustle of any leaves.

Helena looked around to see if there was any movement or approaching darkness out there, but there was nothing. Not a sound, not a sign of life. She took a step forward and took a deep breath before she continued. She had to keep trying, even if it felt strange to be yelling into the silence of the woods. She cupped her hands to her mouth to make the sound louder.

"Tree Witch, come forth to learn about the bargain that we

want to make with you," she said again, this time even more loudly and firmly.

She was asserting herself, or at least she was trying to. It was part of the plan to get the witch's attention. Helena was supposed to make herself sound confident and happy about this bargain we were going to try and make, in order to lure the witch into thinking that we were silly enough to be fooled by her. And Helena was doing a great job, but the witch wasn't coming. Maybe it was all a lie that she would want wine and orange peels, maybe that was just a myth.

Helena took a step forward, slightly away from us to give her room to shout even louder. She rolled her shoulders back and tried to keep sounding confident as she said, "Tree Witch, please, we have something important to share with you."

I wasn't sure what she meant by that, but at this point we would say anything to get her to come out and meet us.

Helena was looking around frantically but there was nothing, so she continued talking into the woods. "We've brought gifts, wine and orange peels, and important information."

This time, there were no echoes. It was like Helena's voice fell after it hit the trees. This made us all uncomfortable, and a chill went down my spine. Something was coming. The air started to shift around us. It felt like the warmth and light was being sucked out of our surroundings. Slowly, things got darker.

"What's going on?" I said quietly to Mikka.

He looked at me and shook his head in disbelief, grabbing Fern's hand. It continued to get darker and darker, until I had to hold Mikka's other hand to know he was still standing there. We all huddled into a group, pushing Fern into the center and putting our backs to her, holding hands to make a strong fortress against whatever was coming. We also crouched low to the ground, to be as close to one another as possible.

I had never experienced darkness like this. It was like I couldn't see my hand in front of my face, like the whole world had caved in and we were in a black hole. Laughter burst out from someone over the sound of our restless breathing. We couldn't see a thing in front of us, we were completely helpless to any outside attack. The Witch could end us all now and we would have no way of fighting back. We couldn't see, which meant we couldn't strike because we didn't know where she was.

The darkness slowly started to lift and we could finally see the surrounding trees. There was now a figure standing just far enough away that I couldn't quite make out what she looked like.

You fools," the Tree Witch said.

Her voice sounded so familiar. She stepped closer, darkness still surrounding her. The figure looked like a human body, which was not at all what I'd expected from the old tales about her kind.

"I can't believe none of you figured it out," she said, stepping closer and lifting the darkness that enveloped her to reveal her true nature.

*Emmeria.*

"How?" I said, shocked at what I was seeing. "Emmeria?" My voice was shaking as I said her name out loud.

"The queen?" Mikka said, also in shock.

"How did you find us?" Helena asked.

"You called for me, did you not?" the queen said. "I'm the Witch, after all." She smirked as she looked at us.

It took me a moment to figure out what was happening in front of me. The queen was the Tree Witch. It didn't make sense. How could she be both?

"Impossible," I said.

Everyone looked shocked except for Kilko. Kilko looked amused.

"I knew," she said. "I knew from the last time we spoke that you were not the same as before."

That was right, Kilko had told us that she thought the queen seemed different, somehow changed. But it didn't make any sense.

"So are you not the real queen?" I said, trying to piece together the information that I'd just learned.

Emmeria burst out laughing and took a step closer. She was wearing a long, draped black cloak with a lacey train that trailed behind her. It covered her jet-black leather bodysuit that fit like armor (it probably was armor), and her dark hair was beautifully tied in a braid that trailed down her back. Her makeup looked like war paint, deep red eyeshadow that stood out among the black of her outfit and hair.

We had all shifted from our protective circle to stand and face her, placing Fern behind us. She saw us move and laughed even harder, almost knocking herself over.

"You cannot be serious," she said. "I don't know how you didn't figure any of this out. I mean, I have been waiting for the day to see little Fern again, and it's just my luck that you end up in my castle all those weeks ago. Even then I thought, they must be playing into this, they must know more than they are letting on. But no? You know nothing? It is quite shocking, quite *amusing*." She let the last word roll off of her tongue.

My heart was racing. It didn't matter anymore what happened after this, any form of backup plan was gone because they all didn't count on the witch being someone we were already running from.

"None of you are leaving this forest today," Emmeria said. "Well, except Fern."

Mikka stepped in front of us all. "You won't touch her," he said, looking into the witch's eyes with death on his mind.

"You have always been brave, dear Mikka," she said. Then she waved her hand to the side like it was nothing. His body flew into a tree and fell to the ground.

"NO!" I shouted.

The air felt like it was completely gone from my body. I had lost too much, too many people I loved. I started to run towards Mikka to check if he was ok, but I was moving in place. The witch's hand was pointed at me, as if she was preventing me from running. I got tired trying to push through it and fell to my knees, out of breath after having gone nowhere. I saw Helena's eyes start to glow and flicker red, saw her clench her fists to try and use the worst of her gifts, but she fell to the ground in exhaustion too.

"Don't bother trying, I am more prepared for this moment than ever," Emmeria said.

Bondi helped pull me up onto my feet and Gregorio grabbed Helena. I turned around to grab Fern's hand.

The black knight stood there, holding Fern in his arms.

"You will not have her!" I shouted.

But he just walked Fern over towards Emmeria. Emmeria laughed again as we all struggled to move forward while she was forcing us to stay in place.

"Since you'll all die shortly, I might as well tell you how I did it," she said with a smug look on her face.

I glanced over at Mikka's still body to see if he was breathing. I could see a shallow breath in and out which made me feel momentarily better.

"How?" Kilko asked. She looked exhausted. "You couldn't use this kind of power when you were on the ship before. So why are you able to use this kind of power now?"

I had thought the same thing: why would she not have used this power before? It looked like everyone in our group was getting the life slowly drained out of them by being stuck in place. It was a gift unlike anything I had ever seen.

"I was waiting for the right moment," Emmeria said. "I needed something more that... well, I'll tell you about it in a little bit. But

I couldn't use my power all at once. After all, I'm half human now, so I had to save this for the right moment."

Emmeria. The queen. The witch. All the same.

"Well, a long while ago, I made a deal with a little baby," she said. "Not that the baby could have had a choice in the matter, but I offered her immortality in trade for part of her human form. This allowed me to shift from a Tree Witch into a human. As a Tree Witch, I was unable to step into the light or I'd perish, so this was the only way to find safety. I went into the Kingdom of Melted Cor, disguised as a spy with information about the king from this kingdom. They let me see the queen and I made it clear that it was of utmost importance that it was just the two of us when I shared the information."

She paced back in forth with her chest out, proud of what she had done.

"Then, when it was just us, just me and that silly queen, I used my powers to enter into her body. What Fern had traded with me allowed me to take any human form, so what better form than that of the queen? I would never have been able to do it without the part of Fern's being that gave me the sequence I needed to enter into the light."

Emmeria looked over at Fern and smiled. Fern looked disgusted.

"So thank you, Fern," Emmeria said. She pointed at the knight. "I let this one in on my secret and ensured him a place at my side if he was completely in my service for eternity." The knight nodded and the witch continued. "I have sat and used this identity of the real Emmeria for years now, but all I wanted it for was to find a way to find that book, Fern, the golden axe, and the last piece to my puzzle." The witch pointed at me. "You."

"Me?" I said, completely confused. "What are you talking about?"

Helena grabbed my shoulder, pulling me back closer to her, Kilko, Bondi and Gregorio.

"You're as surprised as I am, yes," the witch said as she stopped and looked at me. "If I had known who you were when we were at my castle, all of this would have been different, but I didn't until I spoke with the king."

"I– I– I'm not sure what you mean," I stuttered. I tried to take a step back but my body was still frozen in space. I felt the panic attack coming on. There was nothing I could do to stop whatever it was that she was going to try. I knew that these may be our last moments here and I looked over at Mikka, wishing he would wake up just so I could say goodbye.

"I needed the bloodline of your grandfather," the witch said as she paced back and forth. "His gift is the only way to ensure my rule. With the power to turn things to gold, I'll have all authority over currency, and with Fern's human form, I will be able to use the book. You see, with Fern, I can now take the rest of her human form. Unfortunately for her, that will mean her death. I didn't know back then that I would want to become fully human, but I realized that with the book and the golden gift I would be completely unstoppable. The only catch is that I have to be human or Potens in order for the book to work. I didn't know that. I also realized that I would need to find someone that was related to your grandfather in order to access his bloodline and gain his gift. Since the king had taken his head, his body would be of no use, so I needed the next best thing." She stopped pacing and looked right at me.

"But... but I don't have that gift," I said with an unsteady tone, my words stuttering as they fell out of my mouth.

"You see, Evergreen, you do," the witch replied. "Obviously you can't access it, but Potens keep the gifts handed down to them, even if they can't use them. And when I found out that Dova was also your grandmother – jackpot. I knew then that you would be the key to accessing all of that power. Unfortunately for you, you'll also have to die for me to use it." She said it with such certainty in her voice. "I have been growing weaker and weaker in this half-human body. The half-life is draining. I knew I was running out of time, so it was pure luck that you all ran into me when you did."

She smiled like she knew she had won, but then Helena looked over at me with a wink. I wasn't sure why she was giving me a look, but I knew I was missing something important. The witch hadn't noticed though and went on.

"When the king and I spoke, he told me everything I needed to know. We agreed that I would come and get the book for him, by any means necessary, and then I would get to keep Fern. This meant I could have immortality, and he could use the book how he wanted. However... " She slowed and turned to us. "He doesn't know that I have been immortal for a very long time, or that there's no use in me having Fern without the book. He must have thought that I would actually follow his plan, but how wrong he was." She smirked and pulled something that was hooked to her belt loop from behind her back.

It was the king's crown.

"He left it sitting on his table, so naturally I took it. I knew that with this, the book, Fern's human form and your ancestors' gifts, Evergreen, that I would live no longer in the shadows. I would be feared. And, most importantly, in the light."

She placed the crown on her head. It shimmered gold as she looked at us and smiled. My heart raced and raced as I tried not to smile too. She had *stolen* the gold. She had *stolen the cursed crown.* She was now cursed, just like the king, so nothing would ever happen as she wanted it to. Somehow she hadn't seen this coming and I held back my smile. Gregorio and Bondi looked at one another, realizing the same thing.

"Emmeria," I said. "Queen. Tree Witch. Whatever you want to be called. Take me. Leave my friends alone. You don't need to be human if you use me to use the book. I'll do it, and when you need my grandfather's gifts, then you can kill me and find some other human to read the book. You don't need Fern for this. She doesn't need to die."

Mikka was starting to wake up, pushing himself up to sit as he looked around to take in his surroundings. He got slowly to his feet.

"Mikka," I whispered. A huge weight came off my chest as I realized he was alive and, more importantly, that he was ok.

The witch started to laugh. "You would like that, wouldn't you? Here's the problem – you don't have anything to trade that would even be worth that. You don't have anything to give, just your life. Sure, I don't need Fern to be the one to die, but she has some of my powers so I can't let her live."

Her expression turned serious as she looked at Fern. The black knight was still holding Fern tightly. I remembered that he could feel the vibrations of lies and knew that I would have to stretch the truth in order to keep him from sensing that I was not being completely honest. I had to be strong now, I had to be brave. I looked around at Kilko, Helena, Bondi, Gregorio and of course Mikka. My friends. I needed to stop her before it was too late. I needed to stop her from hurting anyone that I loved. I could be brave for them. I could do this.

"I know where the book is," I said. "You can't have it if we're all dead."

The witch looked around for a moment, pondering that thought, before looking at the knight. He nodded. "I could find the book if I wanted to," she said, "but with you I'm sure it will take less time. Bring it to me."

"I'll lead you to the book on one condition," I said. "You let my friends go first."

She let out a loud laugh. "You must think I am stupid, or a fool. If I let them go, they will just come after me. No, I won't be doing that. I will let them live if you show me the book first."

I knew from what I'd been told that Tree Witches were cunning, that they would try and trick you at any moment. I knew that I had to see her as a monster, rather than the form she was wearing in front of us now. I knew that she was lying.

"And how would they be living?" I asked. I knew I had to ask questions to ensure their safety. I was certain she was trying to trick me.

She smirked. "Well, you're smarter than you look, Evergreen," she said. She paced for a moment before answering me. "They will be prisoners for the rest of their lives. They will be fed two meals a day, have comfortable beds and get to live in close quarters with one another."

"They aren't dogs, Emmeria," I said. I took a deep breath and continued. "No, you will let them live in a home together. They won't be chained or anything like that."

I was trying to act convincing. Yes, sure, I wanted to bargain, but realistically I was trying to buy us some time. I needed her to think that I believed we were actually trading, when really I just wanted to lure her to the book and wipe her memory for a bit with my tea. I knew the cursed gold would be messing up anything that she was trying to accomplish, so even if I led her to the well, she would fail. The thought bubbled up inside me as I tried to hide my eagerness.

"Fine. Deal," she said sternly. "But if any of them step a toe out of line, the deal is off."

"Deal," I said, trying to hide that happiness I was feeling knowing that she was about to be fooled.

She would lose.

The knight held Fern while we all walked the long journey back to the well in Kinver. Everyone in our group knew that this would be a good chance to escape, but we were also being pushed by whatever force Emmeria was using on us. It was intense, the kind of power she possessed, and to know that this was only part of it, since she had traded some with Fern, was frightening.

Mikka's hand grazed mine as he was pushed forcibly past me. He looked like he was in pain, and I wanted so badly to hug him and tell him I loved him. I hadn't said that yet but I felt it. I think he knew.

"We're almost there," I said.

The woods started to get less and less dense as we walked closer to the well at the edge of the forest. The top of the well appeared in the distance. I knew this would be our only opportunity to try and escape, but my heart sank as I wondered if this would work.

We made a circle around the well with Emmeria closest to the well.

"Well, where is it?" the witch said.

"It's in there." I pointed down at the well.

She nodded and stepped closer to the well so she could look over and see where it was hidden. She stood for a long moment, looking over at the water. I held my breath for as long as I could, waiting to see if the tea fumes had worked.

"Queen," the black knight said, concerned.

I suddenly felt unshackled by her force, as did everyone else. Kilko and Helena looked at each other and nodded.

"NOW!" they shouted.

The queen turned around, looking really confused. It had worked. Thank the heavens. Kilko and Helena turned to face the knight, Helena's eyes glowed red as she began to shake. The knight let go of Fern as he started to shake too, but not from his own gift, from Helena's. He fell to the ground, his armor clanging against the small rocks and cobblestones beneath him. His helmet fell off, revealing the completely burned face of a man that none of us had ever seen before. Someone must have tortured him. He must have sided with Emmeria because he had only ever known things that were worse than her.

He laid there, lifeless. Helena's eyes were still red. Kilko quickly turned around to put Emmeria, or whoever she was, to sleep and she dropped quickly to the ground. Bondi and Gregorio grabbed her body and tied up her arms. The cursed gold from the crown must have worked because Emmeria hadn't been able to get what she wanted. I had hoped this would work and it had.

"What should we do with her?" I said.

Gregorio looked at me with sad eyes. "I think you know what we have to do," he said.

I couldn't kill her while she lay lifeless on the ground. Sure, the knight was dead but he had been threatening Fern. It just didn't feel right to hurt her as she lay there sleeping.

"No, we can't kill her now," I said pleadingly.

Helena's glowing eyes went back to normal. "What do you mean we can't kill her? She has been ruining our lives, trying to kill us, she kidnapped Fern and wanted to use you as a sacrifice. How on earth are you suggesting we don't kill her?" Helena seemed annoyed with me.

"If we kill her, then we are just like her," I said firmly. "And we are not."

Fern walked up to me and grabbed my hand. "I have an idea," she said.

We all looked at each other, and then at little Fern.

"What's your idea?" I said as I bent down a bit closer to listen to her.

Fern looked back at Mikka. "Well, I'm not sure you're going to like it."

We had been traveling in silence after Fern explained her idea to us. She wanted us to keep Emmeria asleep as we headed back to the castle. She had been having these dreams that she'd thought were nightmares, but she realized now may be similar to mine: path-dreams.

It didn't make sense though. Fern had been around the golden axe for long enough, but no one else was having these path-dreams. I could only guess that Fern's powers were responsible. None of us really understood them just yet, although we now knew they were from the witch.

We were all on horseback, riding towards the castle. We'd decided that it would be best to leave the book in the well for now. We could use it as leverage if we got caught.

"Explain it one more time," I said to Fern. We needed to know as much as we could about this dream.

Fern rode beside me, holding tightly to Helena. "The king is there when I first arrive in the dream. Everyone's looking at him. There's also a dark figure lurking at the side of the room. I try to step closer to see who or what it is, but it's just a mirror. It's like I'm looking at myself, but I'm not me."

I could feel Mikka take the deepest breath he had taken all day. I knew he was extremely overwhelmed by this. None of us knew exactly what it meant, but one thing was certain: Fern could become the darkness, just like that story had said. My heart sunk by what this could mean, that she would no longer be human.

"What's the plan?" Bondi said with a blank expression. I think losing his gift had wounded him in a way where he wasn't quite himself anymore.

"We go in with Emmeria and try to give her up as a prisoner so that the king lets us all go" I said. "He doesn't need Fern anymore if he has the witch. He can use her to take the immortality, if that's what he wants so badly. I think we can also use the book being hidden to try and ensure our safety, so we can have normal lives again."

But Helena and Kilko shook their heads. "He won't change, though," Kilko said. "He will always look down on us Potens. We have to take him down. You heard what Julian said, once someone reads the book, they will do anything to get it back. I'm sorry Ever, but as much as you want things to be peaceful and perfect after this, you have to know that he has to die in order for that to happen."

I felt my shoulders sink, disheartened by this. We didn't have a solid plan to take him down. In fact, we were walking ourselves right back into enemy territory with Fern and Emmeria, even though we knew that they had tried to kill us repeatedly. This all seemed like an awful idea.

"Well then, what's your plan?" Bondi said to Kilko with an attitude. He looked at her with a heated expression. "You want to waltz in there with one human, one Potens that's basically a human, a small child and four other Potens, one of whom has a gift that is completely useless in battle, no offense Evergreen. You want to do that and then what? Fight off an entire army? Kill the king? What's the plan after, huh? What are we going to do when there is no king, no order? Appoint one of us? We've got to think this through. I mean, this whole journey has literally cost a few of us our lives and me my gift. What's it all worth? We can't just waltz in there and try to kill everyone."

Bondi seemed to be the voice of reason. We all knew it had to have been hard to lose his gift like that, something that had meant so much to him for so long. It really was a big part of his identity, but even without it he was still wanting to think things over and find a way to talk through our solutions. It was what made his voice in the matter important.

"You know what, you're right," Helena said. "It has been hard. We've lost friends, we've lost a part of you, but yes, in the end it will be worth it because we're standing up for the right thing. We're standing up for Potens now and in the future. We have to get rid of this king that wants to divide us. You're right, we do have to come up with a plan, but I also think we have to end the king. No matter what."

We rode in silence for another two full days, taking only short stops to rest, rehydrate and eat. We were all still thinking over what Bondi had said, but it was hard to think when each step the horses took led us closer to Crestwood.

Because of the horses we took the long way around the Ridge again and headed straight north after. It would only take us one more full day to get there if we continued moving without sleeping for longer than an hour at a time. This all made me wish that I'd been on horseback when I was first running from the king. It had taken so much longer on foot.

"I think I have an idea," Gregorio said as we rode. "It's crazy, but it's something."

Everyone had been silent for the last two days, trying to think of a plan as we rode. This was the first person to break that silence.

"We're all ears," Kilko said.

"Well, we could set it up exactly like Fern's dream," Gregorio said. "Find a way to the king. If Fern is the darkness, what does that mean for us exactly?" Gregorio said it in a way where he was obviously trying to prompt the answer from us, but knew the answer already himself as well.

"It would mean that she has something we still don't know about," Mikka said cautiously. "That we can use to our advantage?" He clearly still didn't want to put Fern at risk.

"Precisely," Gregorio said. "Fern will be able to do something we're all unaware of. That gives us an opportunity to strike and kill Alco and the king, if they're both there. Then, once we place the king's crown on someone else's head, the guards will have to obey that person and we'll have solved our big problem."

"One tiny problem I see with all of this," Mikka said. "Fern doesn't know how to use her gifts. We're going in there with the main part of this plan being a small child that literally can't control anything. We don't even know what that dream means for her yet."

"I'm not that little Mikka," Fern said quietly from the back of Helena's horse. "I do appreciate you always looking out for me, but I've been through enough and I want to end this."

Helena smiled. She seemed proud that this little girl would not let her age or size stop her from having the courage of a knight.

"I know I can do this," Fern added. "I saw it. And all of Evergreen's dreams came true, so why can't mine?" Her voice got quiet.

"If I have to become the darkness to end this, then maybe that's what's best."

Mikka looked at her with a blank stare. If it was a true path-dream then it would happen, just as she'd imagined it, even if it was a little different. If she'd seen it in a dream, then she could do it.

"I think you're all missing two big problems in this plan," Kilko said, and we all turned to listen to her. "One, we don't know if in that dream Fern has some sort of incredible gift or if she's just seeing something or someone else. We're relying on that detail to be the one thing that helps us, but what if it becomes something different? Something we didn't expect? And two, what on earth makes you think that we would be able to defeat the king and Alco and his Potens guards?"

It was a good point. I wasn't quite sure of that either.

"Here's the thing," Helena said. "We either try and defeat the king and end all of this, or we run and try to live out our lives in fear for the rest of our days. It seems like an easy answer to me."

Kilko rolled her eyes even though she knew Helena was right. Helena was courageous, which sometimes meant being bold. Even when others might not be, she always seemed to be our beacon of strength and I admired her for that, although it may have been a little naive. We knew she was right though.

We had to go to the castle and end this.

The Forest of Embers appeared through the trees. It was easy to spot as the gold reflected on everything. But it was too bright to ride through, and we weren't trying to come into Crestwood undetected. We wanted the king to know we were here.

"Let's follow the tree line to the Kingsway and show ourselves so we don't get ambushed by any of the King's Guard," Gregorio said. He and Kilko were sharing a horse this time.

Bondi nodded and moved to take the lead, with the witch draped over the back of his horse. Kilko had kept forcing her back to sleep each time she'd awoken throughout the ride; it was the only way to ensure our safety. Helena and Fern rode in the center of all of us, since we wanted to keep Fern surrounded.

"There," Bondi said, pointing ahead to the road that ran through the golden forest.

It was just like I remembered it from the last time we were here. Magnificent. The golden leaves crunched under the horses' hooves on the dirt path. The deep breath I took in felt like home, knowing that my grandfather had made this forest. As we rode on, Mikka squeezed my hand. He could sense when my energy started to shift from that calm sensation to panic as we got closer to the castle.

Ahead, we saw four King's Guard riding their horses at us. We'd been able to hear them for a while now, but we could finally see them fully as they approached from the castle and formed a circle around us, stopping us from going anywhere.

"Halt, I command you all," the first guard said to us. "What are you doing in this forest?"

"We're who you've all been looking for. I'm Evergreen, Evergreen Rivers," I said aloud, proud of my family name. "We're here to make a deal with the king."

I swallowed so hard that I think they must have heard it, and nerves filled me. But I had to stay strong right now. We needed to end this.

"Well, well, well, I can't believe you would all come to surrender yourselves," the second guard said.

"I can't believe we're the ones to find them. We're going to get promoted," said the third guard to the other three.

"We're making a deal, you didn't catch us," I said, trying to clarify an important point to them.

"It won't matter what the reason is when we bring you all into the castle," the fourth guard said. "Come with us."

We all looked at each other and nodded, heading out with guards in front and in back toward the castle. We needed to do this. We needed to end this now.

# 25

The castle gates were just as I remembered them. This time though it felt more final, like we had more to lose. We either walked in here and succeeded in our quest, or we didn't. My hands trembled slightly as I held onto Mikka, trying my best to put on a brave face, but I knew that us coming here meant death for either us or for the king. Both were final. Both were permanent. I looked over at Fern, so small and brave. I couldn't stop thinking about her path-dream and what that might mean for us.

The guards on horseback instructed another group of guards to open the gate, and we entered Crestwood once again.

"This way," the front guard said.

He led us down cobblestone paths, through high walls and through the city that Bondi and Gregorio knew from long, long ago. I knew this wasn't easy for Bondi, knowing that he'd lost his gifts in Crestwood, but I also knew that he wanted revenge. And this was the perfect place to get it.

We turned a corner that would lead us to the square, the very place we'd almost died a long while ago. It looked different now.

There was a shimmering, see-through wall that covered the square. As we passed through it, I felt like something in me had changed.

"What was that?" I asked the guard loudly, alerting the others to whatever it was that I'd felt.

The guards looked at each other and smirked. "Alco figured out a way to infuse metal to create a force field that temporarily suspends your gifts," one guard said. "Oh, and it works better than last time," he added with a smile.

"The ring on the ship," Helena said. She tried to flicker her eyes red, but no luck. It was more powerful than the other one, much stronger.

"What? How?" I said with panic in my voice. Helena looked at me with sharp eyes. We were going to die here without any of our gifts.

"Practice is how," said one of the guards, smiling as he pulled his golden mask up. "The first few Potens who were forced to walk through it died. Then the next few just permanently lost their powers. After more practice, we got it right in just a few hours."

I didn't understand how they could be happy about this. They were Potens too. They had to be wearing something that prevented them from being impacted, but we were moving too fast toward the king for more questions. We were here powerless and empty-handed. Someone was going to die, and I had a feeling that this time, it was us.

I couldn't let that thought control me though, we had to try. We had to win, not just for us, but for humanity.

The king stood facing away from us on his stage in the square. I could see his purple suit from here. He had Potens in shackles hidden on the corners of the stage, waiting unwillingly for his command. There were no extra guards other than the four that were with us.

We got too close to the stage for my comfort and the guards said in unison to us, "HALT." Their voices commanded our compliance, and one the guards said with a smile, "King, we have brought you something you will want to see."

The king slowly turned around. His face looked older now, like time and exhaustion had not been kind to him. He looked like he hadn't been sleeping since the last time we were here in this castle. The crown had not done him well. Anxiety filled me as I realized he was no longer cursed by the gold, since it had been stolen from him. I don't know why I didn't think of that until now. We had the physical crown with us, although we hadn't revealed that yet.

"Mikka, Evergreen, Fern, and the rest of you," the king said, "it's so, so good to see you. I can't begin to tell you how good it is to see you all here with me now. I'm so glad to hear of your surrender and continuous servitude to the crown for the rest of your lives."

He spoke as if he was willing it into existence. He must have felt powerful without the curse of the stolen gold. We hadn't stolen it though, so maybe, just maybe, we had a fighting chance.

"We aren't here to surrender, King Jett," I said. "We're here to strike a bargain."

We all jumped off of the horses since it wasn't like we were going to make an escape here this time. Not with that force field up that was making us weaker by the minute. So I took a step closer to him, to try and show him that I was not afraid, even though I was trembling inside.

He raised his eyebrow, as if surprised, and said, "Oh, dear Evergreen, there is nothing I could want from you to change all of your fates. What is it that you had hoped to bargain? I'm curious, I must know." He put his hands behind his back and slowly paced back and forth at the edge of the stage proudly.

"We have the Tree Witch," I said sternly. "The Tree Witch was the Queen of Melted Cor."

He didn't change his expression, just kept pacing for a moment.

He stopped abruptly and turned to face me. "Do you think I didn't know?" he asked, a grin appearing. "You must all take me for a fool. I knew exactly who and what she was. She didn't know that I knew, but I sent her to kill you as part of our deal and I knew you'd lead her to the Book of Viempro. It was easier to have you all walk back in here with everything I needed."

I smiled. "We don't have the book," I said confidently.

A dark, hooded figure appeared from the side of the stage.

*Alco.*

"Ah, my dear, we know you don't have the book," Alco said. "Because we already do." He slid open his robes to reveal the Book of Viempro in his hand.

"How?" Helena said.

I felt my heart drop. This couldn't be possible. I looked around in the square for a mirror, the mirror in Fern's dream, but there was nothing. Fern was also looking around, but her dream may have just been a dream, not a path-dream.

"We knew she would find you all," Alco said, brushing the spine of the book with his hand. "Well, that you would find her. So I followed her, knowing that it would lead me to the book."

"How did you get past my tea?" I said pleadingly.

"Pft. Your gift is pathetic. I drank an antidote before looking for it," Alco said proudly. "I knew you all had to be up to something." He had read from the book and couldn't be without it for too long.

The witch started to move slowly. Kilko tried to use her gift with all her might, but in this place it was gone. The witch slowly slid off of the horse, landing right next to Fern. She was still half-asleep.

"Ah, Emmeria," the king said. "Tree Witch, it is about time that you woke up. Here is what's going to happen. I will take the witch and Fern, to take their eternal life. You will all become prisoners, and we will move on with our lives. Unfortunately, Fern and the witch will have to die, but hey, it's a good deal."

I realized in that moment that only the witch had known she could use my grandfather's gift. The king did not, which meant he wasn't after me. While the thought was comforting, I couldn't let him take Fern to die.

Mikka lunged toward the king, but one of the guards stopped him in his tracks. They all had arrows pointed at us now. This was no longer a bargain, but a surrender. We were all going to die. I pulled Mikka back as Helena, Kilko, Gregorio and Bondi shrunk away from the arrows, trying to distance themselves from the weapons. Fern fell to her knees beside the witch, who had started to open her eyes.

"Fern, come here," Mikka said sternly.

Fern looked at Mikka, at all of us. She then looked back up at the king. "You have got this all wrong," she said.

The king let out a low laugh. "Oh?" He took a step closer to the edge of the stage. "How's that, little Fern?" The clouds rolled in overhead, completely covering the sun. Like a signal that it was all over.

"You are not going to win," Fern said. "Not now, not ever. This is for my family."

Mikka's eyes widened. This was what Fern's dream had meant and we had all only just noticed it. Fern and the witch were looking directly into each other's eyes as the witch came fully awake. With their matched gifts and half of each other's souls, it was like a mirror. Fern looked at Mikka and mouthed, "I love you."

"NO!" Mikka shouted, but it was too late.

Little Fern put her hands onto the witch and, with a gift we didn't know she had, she gave away the rest of her human form, taking all of the witch's dark gifts into herself. Before our eyes, Fern transformed from a human girl into swirling darkness. The force field had no effect on her, as she was not a Potens.

She was a witch. The story came true. She became the darkness.

The guards started releasing their arrows at her, but Fern was just a dark cloud so it wasn't working. The king and Alco stepped back, the king stumbling over his own feet.

"No, please, I'll do anything," he said as he looked into the enormous darkness in front of him.

By now the darkness had swallowed us all completely, blocking out all light. A huge flash of gold struck the king and Alco, knocking the rest of us over. Then, the darkness started to get smaller and smaller again, until it was in a human-like form. It was Fern, but also it wasn't. It was as if the darkness was trying to remember what her form looked like. She looked like Fern, but was slightly transparent and her eyes glowed purple. The clouds slowly started to separate, allowing the sun to shine through, and Fern stepped onto the stage and into the shadows, as if she knew that the sun would cause her harm. The guards stepped back and put down their bows as Mikka ran up onstage to what was now Fern.

"My brave, brave little sister," he said.

We couldn't hug Fern because she wasn't in a solid form anymore, so we all stood around her for a moment. Alco and the king were dead because of Fern's bravery.

Then, I heard a sound from behind me.

"You won't win that easy," a voice said.

The witch had grabbed a sword from one of the Kingsmen and was swinging it right at us. I turned and reached for my golden dagger, pushing Helena to the side just in time to stop her being struck by the sword. Now that the witch was fully human, the weapon was so heavy for her to hold that it was delaying her response. I lunged forward while I had the chance and stabbed her in her black heart. She burst into golden flames and evaporated into the universe.

I fell to my knees, sobbing because I had just killed her. "I didn't want to, but she was going to hurt you," I said to Helena.

Helena smiled, to show me she was proud, and Mikka came rushing over to me. "You had to Ever, you had to," he said as he pulled me to my feet.

"You were brave, Ever," Helena said, patting me on the back.

But I turned to Fern and said, "No, she's the brave one."

Fern had saved us all. The little girl we were so worried about had sacrificed her human form to save us.

"What does it feel like?" I asked Fern. I knew it must feel different. She was a Tree Witch now, an eternal creature and no longer human.

"It feels like I am everything and nothing at the same time," Fern said. "I feel like me, but with no restrictions. It's strange." She shrugged to comfort her extremely worried older brother. "I'll get used to it."

We all knew she would never be normal now, but I guess, in the end, normal is boring. Fern had been through so much in such a short period of time that maybe it was better for her to have more power than anyone else.

"What now?" Bondi said as we looked at the empty throne.

"We need a new king, of course," I said. I pulled the crown out from my bag and held it in my hands. We had to pick someone to pick up the pieces of this broken Kingdom. "I've been thinking about this for a while now, as we traveled. I think the best person to be the king would be you, Bondi. You have been a Potens, and now you live without a gift. What better person to rule the kingdom than someone who has been both Potens and human?"

Helena smiled in agreement while Gregorio nodded happily and enthusiastically. Mikka nodded and Fern gave two thumbs up. Even Kilko nodded and said, "That's not a bad idea."

Bondi looked at the crown I was holding in my hands. "That's a lot of responsibility. I'm not sure that I deserve it. And I don't think I can do it alone." He looked over at Gregorio.

"You'll never be alone when I'm around, brother," Gregorio said.

"I will protect you," Fern's soft little voice said from the shadows, tucked away from the sun.

Mikka nodded. He knew that this was her calling now, it made sense for her to protect the king. It was hard to imagine that she had more power than anyone on this earth tucked into her seven-year-old self. If I hadn't seen it with my own eyes, I probably wouldn't believe it.

"Everyone in agreement?" I said to the group.

Bondi would be the most understanding to everyone's problems now. He'd had both a gift and none in his lifetime. And since he and Gregorio lived here so long ago, there would be people that they could relate to. It made the most sense. Everyone nodded.

I handed the crown over to Gregorio so he could place it atop his brother's head. Bondi bowed forward to him as the fallen King's Guard slowly got up.

"I will gladly accept this until we can hold a proper election to ensure that this is what the Kingdom wants too," Bondi said. Gregorio nodded.

"Bondi, I am honored to announce you as our new king," Gregorio said as he lowered the crown onto Bondi's head. "The King of Aureum Ignis."

We all lowered ourselves to our knees, including the entire King's Guard who came out from the castle surrounding us. We all bowed out of respect and honor for our new king.

We all stood inside the castle while the guards released the imprisoned Potens. Bondi had started getting to work right away, trying to right the wrongs of the last king. He wanted to prove he was worthy of the title, that he would make everything better, and because the crown wasn't stolen anymore, it would work for him. It had returned to a worthy king. No more cursed gold. There was a lot of commotion and happy shouts as Bondi started implementing ways to spread the news that it was safe to be both Potens and human.

I stood looking out one of the glass windows in the castle, Mikka standing just behind me.

"Well, what will we do now?" I whispered to him, smiling as I watched all of the prisoners running free.

"Hmm, well, I don't know," he said, leaning in to me, "but I do know one thing. Whatever we do, we get to be together. I love you."

He kissed me. It was the first moment we'd had together where we weren't running from danger.

I smiled and hugged him. "I like the sound of that. I love you too."

Home. It felt like home with Mikka. It felt like home with my friends. It didn't matter what came next, as long as I had them.

**FIVE YEARS LATER**

I was woken up to the sound of the new teapot Mikka had given me for my birthday. I could hear him quickly hurrying to move it off the stove, followed by the pouring of hot water into a mug and the quick stirring of a spoon.

"Ever, darling, wake up!" he shouted from the other room. "Tea's ready."

I rolled over a few times, to stretch out after my deep sleep, before calling, "Coming, sweetheart." I rolled off the bed and stretched my arms overhead.

I had more now than I could have ever asked for. We had a cabin, just outside of the Forest of Embers, on the outskirts of the Sunken Forest. Mikka was able to head out into the forest and hunt, and I was able to brew healing teas. It was away from a lot of people to have our privacy, but close enough to go into Crestwood every day to help our king, our friend, Bondi. He was elected King by the people after just a year of trying to restore the Kingdom.

Mikka was on Bondi's board of trusted advisors now, working closely with him to help make decisions on how to keep peace in the kingdom. I, meanwhile, had opened a new tea shop in Crestwood. It was a little bigger than my old one and was getting great business. Ever since Bondi had become king and reopened Crestwood for people to live there, the city was always filled with the noise of people shopping and exploring the tons of markets throughout.

I needed to start getting ready soon and get my shop open, a thought that excited me. I sat up and looked out the window, thinking of our life now, how lovely it was, what we all had gone through to get here.

Little Fern, who was not so little, had saved us all those years ago, which had led us to this moment. Fern now lived at the castle, as a protector to all. The witch had said that she would always live in darkness, and it was true that Fern wasn't able to step into the light anymore. She had to stay hidden in the shadows. But living in the castle and being its protector meant that Fern would always have a place to stay and a purpose, an important one. She had grown so much since it all happened, and she was now able to harness power unlike any I'd ever seen. But, most importantly, she was happy.

I thought often about all the people who helped us on this journey. Dova, Selinda, and Julian. We couldn't have this life without their help all those years ago.

"Ever, the tea is going to get cold," Mikka said.

I laughed. "I'm coming, I'm coming," I shouted.

I rolled out of bed and grabbed the paper that Mikka must have put next to me. It was yesterday's edition – he must have grabbed it when he came home from work. The front page was a picture of all of us from that day five years ago when Bondi was crowned king. The headline read FIVE YEARS OF BUILDING THE KINGDOM BACK.

Helena and Kilko were there smiling on the cover. They had moved into a loft near one of the city's most bustling markets. They both worked as King's Guard for Bondi, both with gifts and courage unlike anyone else.

I looked more closely at the picture. Bondi looked so nervous with his new crown on, but Gregorio was standing there like a very proud brother. He was now Bondi's most trusted advisor, the king's right hand. Gregorio helped Bondi make any decisions as the king continued his mission of repairing the kingdom, implementing

Potens and human connections, and using everyone's gifts-whether actual gifts or just talents- to make the kingdom a better place.

And Mikka and I had our little cabin, that I couldn't have even dreamed of before. We had a small porch where we could look through the trees of the Sunken Forest on one side, and the bright Forest of Embers on the other. The forests I loved so much. We also had a small garden just outside that produced delicious vegetables, and a tree right by the house covered in apples.

I walked into the main area of the cabin. "Hello, darling," I said as I walked over to give Mikka a kiss and grab my mug.

We both walked outside to sit on the porch together and enjoy our tea. Sitting in our wicker rocking chairs, with our tea in our hands, we looked into the forest. I looked over at Mikka and smiled.

Home. I was home.

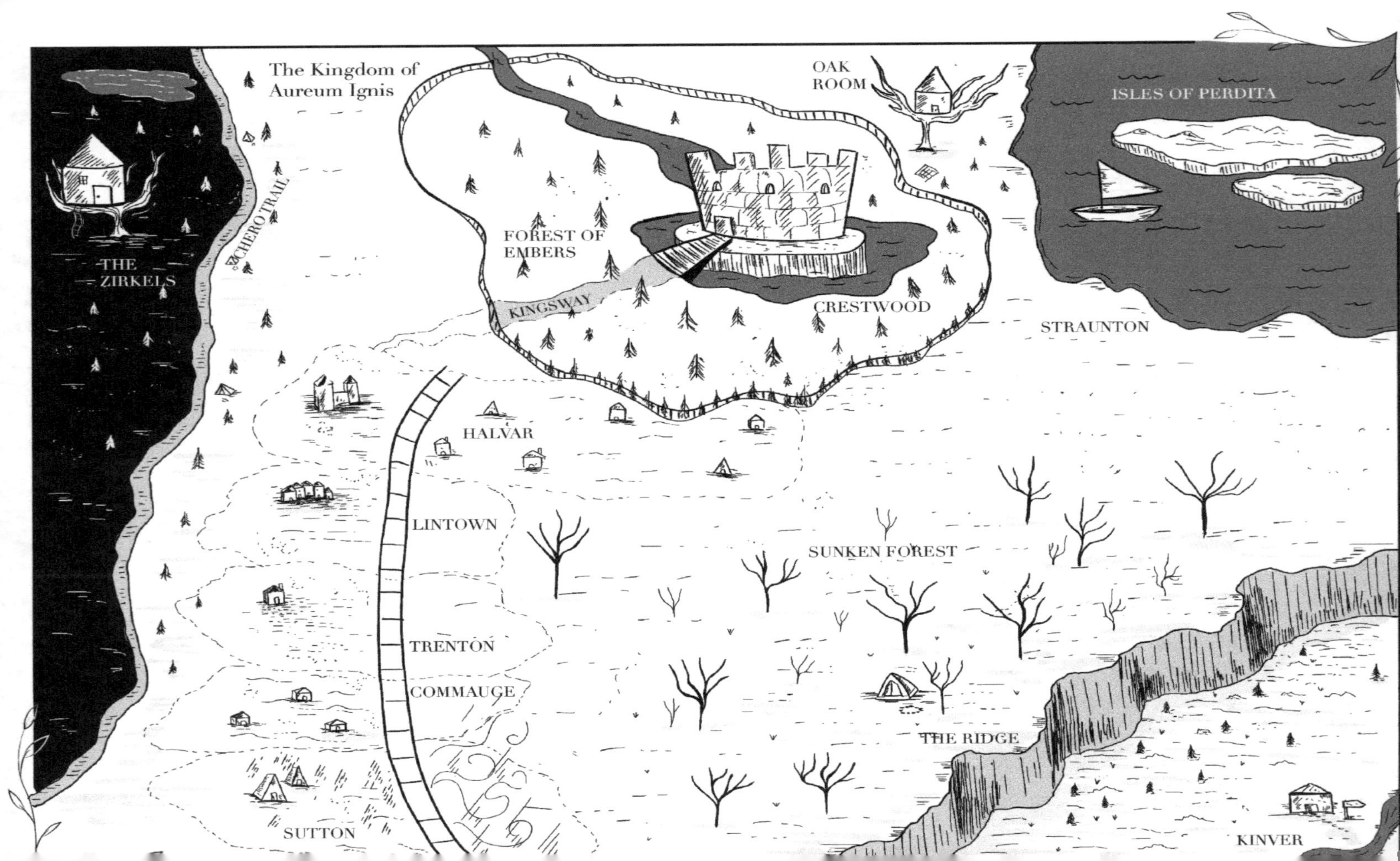
The Kingdom of Aureum Ignis
OAK ROOM
ISLES OF PERDITA
THE ZIRKELS
CHERO TRAIL
FOREST OF EMBERS
KINGSWAY
CRESTWOOD
STRAUNTON
HALVAR
LINTOWN
SUNKEN FOREST
TRENTON
COMMAUGE
THE RIDGE
SUTTON
KINVER

**Kaitlyn Mueller** was born and raised on Long Island, New York. Her love for the outdoors inspired her to move to Colorado where she spent the last 6 years camping, hiking, and backpacking in her free time. Her love for reading has driven her to write her own fantasy series. She currently resides with her Husband in Northwestern Colorado with their dog Blue.

9 798985 334524